The Magician's Apprentice

The Magician's Apprentice

BY SIDNEY AND
DOROTHY ROSEN

Carolrhoda Books, Inc./Minneapolis

Adventures in Time Books

LIBRARY OF CONGRESS CATALOGING-IN-PUBLICATION DATA

Rosen, Sidney.
The magician's apprentice / by Sidney and Dorothy Rosen.
p. cm.
Summary: In 1264, Jean of Toulouse, a young French student and friar accused of heresy by the Inquisition, is sent to Oxford to spy on the scholarly monk, Roger Bacon, who is suspected of being a heretic for his advanced scientific ideas.
ISBN 0-87614-809-7
1. Inquisition—Juvenile literature. 2. Bacon, Roger, 1214?-1294—Juvenile literature. [1. Inquisition—Fiction. 2. Bacon, Roger, 1214?-1294—Fiction. 3. Middle Ages—Fiction.] I. Rosen, Dorothy. II. Title.
PZ7.R7187Mag 1994
[Fic]—dc20
93-10781
CIP
AC

Manufactured in the United States of America

1 2 3 4 5 6 I/BP 99 98 97 96 95 94

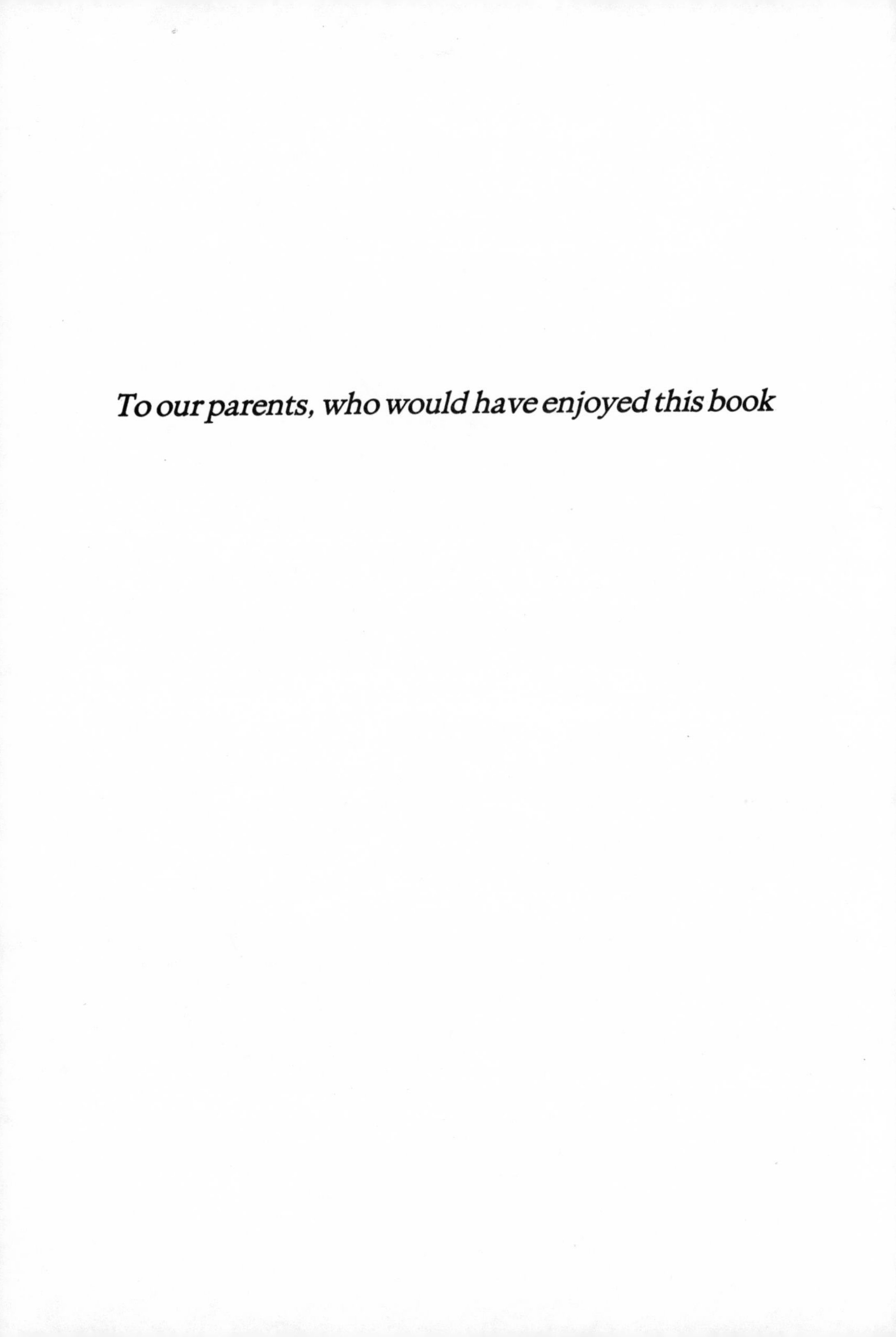

To our parents, who would have enjoyed this book

PREFACE

It's hard to imagine how powerful the Christian Church was during the 13th century. The pope, leader of the Church of Rome, had the same divine power as emperors and kings—the power of life and death over all his followers.

During the 13th century in Europe, science was still mixed with magic and superstition. Moreover, it was dangerous to have ideas which were different from or against the teachings of the Church. Any such idea was called *heresy*. By this time, the Church had set up a special group, called the Holy Office, to handle problems of heresy. This office became known as the Inquisition.

Roger Bacon, a Franciscan monk and professor at Oxford University in England, was a real person. He was a scientist whose ideas were hundreds of years ahead of his time. His vision of experimental science made people suspect him of practicing black magic—that is, controlling or changing nature by making a pact with the forces of evil.

Bacon also revealed the secret of gunpowder to the Western world. He also realized what would happen if the right kind of scientific thinking took place—the coming of advanced technologies. Yet, for hundreds of years, Bacon was thought of as a sorcerer and magician.

This is a fictional story about Roger Bacon and his times, told by a narrator invented by us. As authors often do, we have changed history a bit. Bacon was imprisoned by his own order of monks—not by the Inquisition—and unfortunately, languished there for some years.

CHAPTER ONE

I had just passed my fifteenth birthday when my abbot called me in and handed me the terrifying summons: *You are hereby ordered to appear before the Grand Inquisitor of the Holy Office of Toulouse on the 23rd day of July in this year of Our Lord, 1264....*

There were more words to read on the page, but for a moment they all swam together. The abbot's study suddenly became stifling, and my robe stuck to me. The chant of a group of brothers at their morning devotions in the chapel echoed mournfully in my ears like a dirge. The Grand Inquisitor? What could he possibly want with me? Someone must have made a ghastly mistake!

The abbot's gloomy expression was not comforting. His eyes were studying me as if he had never seen me before, even though I had been living in the abbey these six years.

"But—but what does it mean?" I could hardly get the words out. "What have I done?" To be called before the Inquisitor of the Holy Office! As far as I knew, only those guilty of the most awful heresies against the Church were summoned. And the punishments dealt them—excommunication from the Church, torture, even death. A chill of fear chased up my spine.

He shook his head. "I am not at liberty to say, Jean. They will tell you in their own way. You will report tomorrow at the second canonical hour." His usually open expression seemed closed and guarded. "And you are not to speak of this to anyone. Just carry on your duties as usual—work is the greatest comfort." The abbot gestured with his hand. I was dismissed.

The second canonical hour meant prime—after matins. So I would not know the reason for the summons until twenty-four hours had passed. Twenty-four hours stretched ahead like twenty-four years. The hardest part would be pretending before the others that this day was like every other. Even in normal times, long periods of meditation were hard for me; I had often been accused of too much liveliness. And now I could not even tell my best friend, Paul, about the terrifying appointment facing me.

Maybe the abbot was right, maybe work would help untie the knot of misery in my stomach. And obedience, we had been taught, was the most important of our three vows, because then poverty and chastity would follow naturally. The three knots in the rope around my waist were there to remind me of the vows. Anyway, this was the hour for me to weed my section of the vegetable garden. Here at the abbey, we raised all our own food. Later, there would be the barns to clean. I got my summer work hat of straw and went out to dig up nettles.

Except for the drone of bees, the garden was quiet. Way down at the other end, I could see Paul's broad back. He was tending the grapevines. I hoped he wouldn't notice me. All I could think was, what did I do? I had never spoken a word against my Church or the abbey in my life. Or did I say something in a mindless joke? And who reported me? The strong sunlight from the cloudless sky seemed to burn me through the thin summer robe. Was it just a rumor, or did the Inquisitors really burn people at the stake?

Quick as a serpent's tongue, the thought of running away flickered through my head. It would be so easy to saunter through the gate, dash across the grassy slope of the hill, and lose myself in the dense forest. But where would I go, in my friar's robe and penniless? What did I know of life beyond the monastery walls? Besides, I could not believe that my Church would unfairly accuse a loyal follower like me. Whatever the matter was, it would soon be cleared up. After all, I was innocent.

The odor of the fertilizer we had spread so generously at the planting had never bothered me before. Today it made my stomach feel queasy. All the stories I had heard about the punishments handed out by the Holy Office spun about in my head. Every friar knew that only a dozen years ago, Rome had given the Grand Inquisitor of Toulouse permission to use instruments of torture to force heretics to confess their sins.

If becoming an orphan as a baby was a sin, I was guilty. My parents had died of the marsh fever, leaving me in the care of my mother's brother, Uncle Lucien, and his wife, Aunt Gemma. My aunt told me once that my mother and father had looked forward eagerly to my coming—their first-born child. "You get your blue eyes and fair hair from your mother," she'd said, "but you're tall like your father." She shook her head. "Let's hope you didn't inherit his reckless ways. Whatever possessed him to go farming in those damp lowlands!"

It was generous enough of the two to take me in. I did not come to them with a dowry, as a bride would have, or an inheritance. They had four children of their own, on a tiny patch of farmland. They treated me well, but somehow I always felt that I didn't really belong.

One day, Uncle Lucien took me aside and pointed out that becoming a monk would solve my situation. The day he left me, a worried nine-year-old, at the Dominican abbey, he tried to cheer me up. "Mind you, the friars are

kind. You will have enough to eat and a roof over your head. Your dear mother—my sister in heaven—will bless me for bringing you here. It wasn't easy to get you in, Jean, you know we had to save up for the donation. Work hard and obey your elders. You're a bright lad, you'll get along."

And after the first homesick weeks, I did get along. These six years at the abbey had been good ones, and now I was no longer a novice. I had passed my probationary period with flying colors and had taken my vows. The brothers taught me Latin and Greek, arithmetic, and music. I learned the art of printing letters in the scriptorium, the room where books were made. It was also the library, my favorite place of all.

Unfortunately, only a fraction of my time was free for books. The abbey was a hard-working community. Apart from time spent for devotions, meditation, and learning, we each had a complete roster of daily duties. This meant, besides sweeping and scrubbing the floors and cleaning the latrine and the barn, we helped bake the bread and press the grapes for wine. During the harvest season, we all pitched in to help fill the granary. God gave us muscles and we must use them, the abbot would say. In the workshops, we made our own furniture as well as our daggers and the scabbards to sheathe them. Nobleman, peasant, or friar, every man had to be able to defend himself. The world outside the abbey could be dangerous and violent.

Apparently, I had a good head for words, and the abbot took notice. In fact, only a month before the summons came, he had sent for me. His thinning fringe of hair was turning white, and his skin was seamed and mottled with the brown spots of aging. He was never overbearing, even when scolding us, and his punishments were never harsh or cruel. "Penance should help men become what they ought to be, not crush their wills," he once explained.

Seated at his writing table, the abbot hadn't wasted words. "Jean, how would you like to go to the University of Paris for further training?"

The University of Paris! It was what I'd been dreaming of. Scholars like Thomas Aquinas, known the world over, lectured there. And our Dominican order was in charge.

"There is a scholarship available," he went on, "and we have agreed that you are our most promising young scholar. Though at times we have questioned whether your deportment is serious enough." He pursed his lips.

I blushed. Silent hours were always a trial for me. While trying my hardest to concentrate on the prescribed lesson for the day, I might turn my head and catch one of the elders snoring softly. Then a knowing grin and waggling eyebrows from Paul, who'd noticed also, would be enough to send me into a stifled burst of laughter. Of course Paul never got caught; it was I who had to do penance. All too soon, I earned the reputation of being given to what Brother Sextus referred to as "godless tomfoolery."

"This scholarship," the abbot went on, "will cover your fees, room, and meals for the duration of your degree program. And I think we can add a bit to take care of travel expenses, too. But you'll have to count your pennies with care." He cleared his throat. "And from now on, remember that we expect you to be a model for the younger boys in the abbey. Several of the brothers argued that you were not mature enough to take on the challenge of the university. But I think otherwise. Remember, it would be a sin in God's eyes to waste your gifts in the pursuit of folly. I am putting my trust in you, Jean."

Thrilled by the scholarship, I had assured the abbot that he would not be disappointed in me. Blissfully, I pictured myself striding into the Great Hall of the university to hear Thomas Aquinas speak. I could hardly wait to send word of my good news to my uncle and aunt. Surely my mother and father in heaven were rejoicing with me, too.

So the arrival of the summons from the Holy Office came as a bitter blow. Suddenly I was in disgrace, and I did not even know why.

Early next morning, after an endless night, I stood all by myself, facing a huge desk in the cavernous underground room where I had been told to wait for my interview. Though I tried to put on a brave face, my knees were trembling under my robe. Tales of the instruments of torture whirled in my brain. To occupy myself, I took stock of my surroundings.

Even though a small fire flamed in the fireplace, the

great room felt chilly. It was hard to believe it was July. The wooden wall that faced me was hung with a huge tapestry depicting the death of one of the saints. Such was my state of mind that I couldn't even recall his name. But the body pierced with arrows was not reassuring. Behind the desk were five handsome, high-backed chairs with ornately carved arms. The only sounds were the hissing of the fire and an occasional shuffling in the corridor. The smoke of the fire didn't quite cover the musty aroma, which was like that of a cellar or a place where the sun never shines.

A sudden sound made me jump. Through a side door strode a man wearing the red robe and matching hat of a cardinal—the Grand Inquisitor. Behind him filed four men, dressed in the robes of Dominicans. Deliberately, with expressionless faces, they seated themselves, the cardinal in the center, and stared at me.

Would I remain standing there motionless throughout eternity?

A young monk hurried in, handed the cardinal a piece of parchment, and left. Not a word was spoken.

I had never felt so alone in my life.

The cardinal glanced down at the sheet of parchment and then looked at me. "What is your name?" His voice was deep and solemn, as if giving a funeral oration. Bushy black eyebrows stood out in a long face pitted by the pox.

I had to swallow before answering him. My throat was dry.

"Where do you live?"

"The Abbey of Toulouse, Your Eminence." I shifted from one foot to the other.

"How old are you?"

"Just turned fifteen, Your Eminence." My voice sounded high and squeaky in my ears. Why was he asking these questions? Surely they knew all about me.

"Do you know why you are here?"

I shook my head no.

"Do you know what the word *heresy* means?"

Oh, yes. I nodded my head.

"Tell us how you interpret the word *heresy*, Brother Jean."

"It means you believe in ideas that are against Church laws and teachings."

"Good. Then you understand that to be accused of heresy is a very serious matter?"

"Yes, Your Eminence."

"And you still insist that you do not know why you have been called before the Holy Office?"

I shook my head. "No, Your Eminence, I have no idea."

"Things would go better for you if you were to confess your heresy now."

"Your Eminence, I have committed no heresy that I know of."

"Ah. Perhaps this will refresh your memory." He picked up the sheet of parchment from the desk. "This

was found on the shelf over your pallet in the dormitory of the abbey and handed over to us by a faithful brother." He held out the sheet to me. "Take it." I did so with a shaking hand. "Read what it says."

The moment I saw the first line of print, I knew I was doomed. It was the piece of parchment I had found lying on my shelf the other night. The words had made no sense to me, and I had decided to bring it to Father Guillaume, the abbey librarian. But between duties and the summons to the abbot's office, I had forgotten all about it.

"Read it aloud!" the cardinal commanded.

The four silent listeners stirred and leaned forward.

I moistened my lips and began haltingly. "The only way to fight superstition and fear is to reach a true understanding of how nature works. A good beginning is to understand that God cannot make something out of nothing. But we see things happening on earth and in the sky that we cannot explain, and out of fear we say that what is going on is the will of God...."

"Stop!" The Inquisitor's fist crashed down on the table. "Enough! God can do anything He wants!" He reached over and snatched the parchment from my hands. "Do you deny that this blasphemous writing was in your possession?"

"Yes—no—I mean—"

He cut me off. "Ah, so it's true! I suppose you have an explanation?" His tone was heavy with sarcasm.

"No, no, Your Eminence!" Alarm made the words tumble out. "That parchment—I don't know anything about it."

"Are you implying that the parchment was not on your shelf? That the brother who found it was lying?"

Who dared question the truthfulness of the Inquisition? "No, Your Eminence, not at all. But there must be some mistake. I—I can't imagine how it got there."

His fist crashed on the desk again. "What you imagine or can't imagine is of no significance! The fact that this piece of heretical nonsense was found where it was condemns you, Jean of Toulouse!"

"But—but Your Eminence—" I was babbling, but I couldn't stop. "I swear I know nothing of this matter! I've been a faithful servant of the Church these six years now! I swear by Saint Dominic—"

"Ah," he interrupted, "you swear, do you?" He leaned back in his chair and laid the piece of parchment on the desk before me. The ghost of a smile flickered across his face. "Tell me, Jean of Toulouse, are you willing to swear on the Holy Book that what you have just assured us is the truth?"

He believed me! "Oh, yes! Oh, it is, Your Eminence!"

The cardinal pulled open a drawer and took out a little bell, which he shook. The tinkling brought the young monk bustling in. "Fetch the Holy Book, Brother Julian."

When the great Bible was brought in, I placed my hand on it and repeated the oath. Then the Inquisitor nodded

to the four others and they all left, followed by Brother Julian in the rear, grasping the heavy book in his two hands like Moses bearing the tablets of the Ten Commandments.

Then there was to be no torture? I took a deep breath. Was the ordeal over?

The Inquisitor rose and handed me the parchment. Did he want me to read more? His voice was stern. "Burn it!" He waved an arm at the fireplace.

I did what he ordered. The edges of the parchment grew brown, then black. The sheet curled and shriveled to ash.

"Come here, Jean, we are not finished. You may sit down." He motioned to the chair next to his. "Did you know what you were reading?" I shook my head. "It was written by a pagan atheist, a certain Lucretius of Rome, hated by his own people for his godlessness."

"I didn't realize—"

"Never mind, we shall look elsewhere for the heretic who printed this. Burning in the fire is a proper ending for such filth. Still, the document was found in your possession. Do you admit that?"

To argue was useless. I nodded.

"Well, perhaps you have learned a lesson." His sharp eyes studied me. "Still, the abbot has high praise for your quickness of mind. And the Holy Office has need of such skill." He pressed his fingers together and studied them for a second.

What was he getting at? "But, Your Eminence, I have been awarded a scholarship to the University of Paris—"

"Ah, yes, we are aware of that. But you realize that you must do penance for your sin of foolishness."

So I was to be punished after all.

"We want you to perform a special mission for your order, a mission that will require great skill and cunning." His thin lips curved in a smile. "You will have your scholarship, but not for Paris. Instead, you will attend the University of Oxford."

"But that's in England!" A foreign land. Far from my native France.

"True, but it's a great institution, Oxford. Of course, it is governed by the Franciscan order. But we Dominicans have a chair of law on the faculty there. Naturally, we expect you to be as devoted to your studies as you would be at Paris. But there is an additional task." He cleared his throat. "We cannot speak of it as yet. But before you leave, your abbot will give you sealed orders. The mission on which we are sending you is of utmost importance to our order. Absolute secrecy is vital. You are not to discuss this matter with anyone."

He shook his finger at me. "Remember, the Holy Office has ears and eyes everywhere. If you fail to fulfill the obligations in any way, you will of course forfeit your scholarship. And both you and your family will be accountable to the Holy Office." His eyes burned into mine. "Have I made myself clear?"

I stammered that I understood. He held out his hand for me to kiss the large ring on his index finger. Then I was dismissed.

At least I was not headed for the torture chamber, I told myself as I slowly walked back upstairs. But my brain felt numb. England? A secret mission that needed the cunning of a fox? Even the fate of my good uncle and aunt placed on my shoulders?

A scrap of parchment had changed my whole life.

CHAPTER TWO

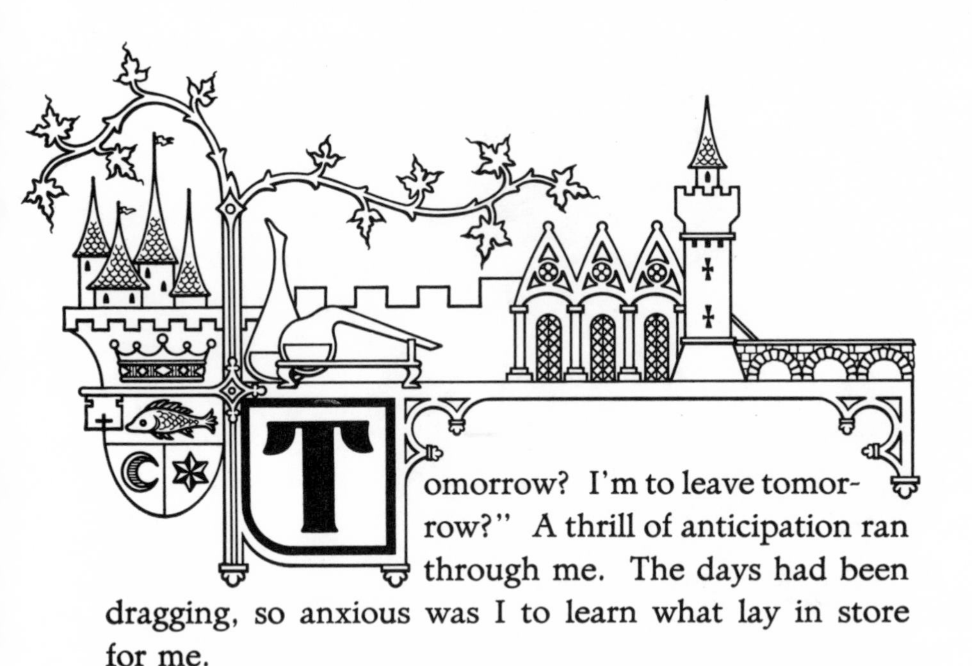

"Tomorrow? I'm to leave tomorrow?" A thrill of anticipation ran through me. The days had been dragging, so anxious was I to learn what lay in store for me.

The abbot nodded. "This may be our last meeting for a long while, Jean." He sighed. When he spoke again, his voice was brisk. "As I was saying, you are to depart at sunrise tomorrow. A horse will be ready for you at the gate. Four of the brothers will accompany you to Paris. It's a long journey, much too dangerous for you to make alone. At Paris, the brotherhood will supply a guide

to take you to Calais, and you'll stay overnight at the monastery there. From Calais, you go by ship to Dover. The abbey at Dover will supply you with transportation to Oxford. Now, is that clear?"

"Yes, Father. But there's one thing—I wouldn't want to leave without first seeing my uncle and aunt."

"Of course. And I've already told the brothers that you'll be stopping off at the village of Grenade to bid your family farewell. You would not want to go so far without visiting them, of course. They took you in as an infant, you must always remember them in your prayers." He picked up a small leather purse from the table. "There is enough here for food and small necessities." He handed me the purse. "If you count your pennies, it should last you the journey. Remember, we are not interested in material possessions except to aid the needy. Even our blessed Saint Dominic was not too proud to ask for alms. Never forget your vow of poverty."

"Thank you, Father, I won't forget." I tied the purse carefully to the belt under my robe, between my crucifix and the scabbard of my dagger. "Are you disappointed with the change of plans? You did want me to go to Paris. And I give you my word, Father, that I know absolutely nothing of—"

The abbot held up his hand. "Not another word, Jean. We must not contradict the authority of those who are our superiors. Nor question the Almighty in his wisdom." He sighed deeply. "Of course, Oxford is

dominated by Franciscans. You'll have to watch out for them, Jean. They tend to pick up new ideas too easily. They don't stop to ask themselves if such ideas might be dangerous for the Church. We Dominicans are never in a hurry to change things. We stand fast to old traditions. So be on your guard." He passed the back of his hand over his brow. "But we must admit that Oxford does have a reputation for fine scholarship."

"I'll do my best. I'll work hard."

He nodded. "That I know. Now, one more matter." He pushed a folded packet across the table at me. "Your assignment. Mind you, to be opened only by our brother at Oxford, who will contact you. He'll explain exactly what your duties are to be."

There it lay, looking innocent enough. The packet was actually a piece of parchment folded and closed tightly with sealing wax. My heart beat faster as I picked it up. I could just make out the symbol of the Holy Office on the seal. Did the abbot know the contents?

He had me repeat the itinerary and the details of the journey. Then he bade me Godspeed.

There was a lump in my throat as I tried to thank him for the years of caring. With all my heart I hoped that he, at least, believed in my innocence.

Back in the dormitory, I packed my few possessions. My woolen robe for winter, undergarments, a pair of sturdy sandals, all made here at the abbey. Brother Robert, who was in charge of the scriptorium, had already given me a wonderful going-away present—a small copy of Saint Mark's Gospel. A book was something I never dreamed of owning—this was worth more than gold to me. The sealed packet I tucked into my bag last.

After vespers, everyone crowded around to say good-bye and tell me how lucky I was to be going all the way to Oxford. A pang went through me at the thought of leaving all my friends; some of us had grown up together. Especially Paul. We had shared so many confidences that a longing grew in me to tell him about the packet. But would the knowledge get him into trouble? Better not tell him. We walked back together to the dormitory.

Lying on his straw pallet next to mine, the last words Paul muttered before falling asleep were, "They say that in the hills of England lives a tribe of two-headed monsters. Take care they don't have you for supper, Jean...." The others called out good-natured warnings, too, and the room was full of muffled laughter. But in no time there were only the sounds of sleep in the darkness.

Only for me, sleep would not come. It wasn't just the excitement of the journey, it was the contents of the packet. Could I travel all the way to England with such an uneasy mind? But to touch the packet would be to violate the vow I had taken so long ago—the vow of obedience. Go to sleep, Jean, I told myself. And finally I did.

The first cock's crow woke me. There was just light enough to make out the shapes around me. As soon as

my eyes opened, I knew what had to be done. I jumped up, went to the bag, and pulled out the packet. Then I hesitated for a minute, remembering the abbot's instructions. What harm would it do if I learned the contents right now? Not knowing what lay in store for me was the real torment. My fingers itched to tear it open. How could I manage to wait through the long journey ahead?

Perhaps if I prayed hard for strength, I could force myself to obey the abbot's orders. I knelt, closed my eyes, made the sign of the cross, and implored our patron saint for patience.

Good Saint Dominic, stand by me and guide me. Help me to be strong, to resist temptation. It's so hard for me to wait to find out what they want of me! The abbot is such a good man, let me be obedient to his wish. Help me to leave the packet untouched.

Finally my eyes opened. The room was growing lighter. The packet was sticky in my hot clutch. My flesh burned as though beset by a fever. It was no use. Perhaps I was a born sinner after all, as the Holy Office seemed convinced. Or just plain reckless like my father, as Aunt Gemma had feared. But to wait one second longer was impossible. Scrambling to my feet, I seized my dagger. With the point I carefully pried the seal away from the parchment. A sudden noise startled me. Was someone awake and watching?

Looking about in a panic, I realized that the noise was only a snore. All the others seemed to be still fast asleep.

Still, one might be pretending; after all, someone had already informed on me. And it was getting later. Tiptoeing to the heavy door that led outside, I pushed it slowly open so it would not creak, and stepped out. The sky was changing from black to the gray that comes just before sunrise. My fingers shook as I opened the parchment and began to read.

"Thomas of York, this letter is being carried by our Dominican brother, Jean of Toulouse, about whom you were informed previously. You are to inform him of his task—getting into the good favor of Friar Roger Bacon so that he may gather evidence of the practice of black magic and devil worship. Remind this brother that what he is being asked to do is only a mild penance for the sin of having heretical writings in his possession. He is to hand over to you any evidence he obtains about Friar Bacon's foul deeds. If you judge Brother Jean's performance to be unworthy in any way, you are to notify us at once. He himself has been warned of the dire consequences of failure. It is vital that this entire mission be kept in the strictest secrecy. This letter is to be destroyed."

My heart sank. This was far worse than I had expected. Now I was to become that creature most despised of all at our abbey—a tattletale. But I had taken the vow of obedience. There was no choice except to obey. After all, I'd be fighting a battle for my own order—and at that, I couldn't help feeling a shiver of excitement. And who was this man Bacon?

A glint of sunlight on my hand snapped me out of my trance. Hastily I refolded the letter, crept back to the dormitory, and stuck it into my pack. The sleepers were beginning to stir. There was barely time to splash my face with water from the pitcher and get dressed. As I snatched up my pack, the bells began ringing for matins, the first canonical hour.

My four companions of the road were already waiting at the gate, their horses pawing at the ground impatiently. They were some of the older friars I had never known well.

"It's late, Brother Jean," one of them snapped. "High time we got started."

The five of us knelt together, said a brief prayer, mounted our horses, and were off to the north. What struck me as strange was that my fellow travelers arranged themselves so that two of them rode on each side of me. Were they just fellow travelers, or were they really my keepers? Did the Grand Inquisitor expect me to bolt? Or maybe I was imagining things; maybe their formation meant nothing.

In no time, we reached a high rise of ground, and the little village of Grenade was spread out before us. Here I led the way. My uncle's small farm was on the outskirts. In the clear light of morning, the farmhouse looked shabbier and more weather-beaten than I remembered; the winter had been harsh. But the greetings from my uncle and aunt could not have been warmer, and my four

cousins—two girls and two boys—hugged me soundly, past rivalries long forgotten. They welcomed the Brothers heartily, too, and soon a generous meal—bread warm from the oven, mild goat's cheese, fresh grapes and apples—was spread on a large cloth laid on the grass under a sheltering tree. The aroma of the grass was pungent and sweet, and every hillock and clump of trees was familiar to me.

"Eat, Jean, eat!" urged chubby Aunt Gemma, her round, ruddy face full of concern. She turned to my lanky, bearded uncle. "Just look at him, Lucien—all bones! And who knows what kind of food those barbarian English eat!"

Everyone laughed. We ate and chatted. My cousins grew round-eyed when I spoke of Oxford. Uncle Lucien left and reappeared with a flagon of ale, and Aunt Gemma filled the mugs that were passed around for a toast. "A bright future for our Jean!" proclaimed my uncle, and my aunt added, "Amen." Then she said, half to herself, "Who knows when we'll ever see him again!"

All too soon, my companions signaled that it was time for us to be on our way. And of course, my relatives had to get back to work in the fields of millet and barley. My uncle's voice was husky when he said good-bye, and sudden tears shone in my aunt's eyes. Long after we'd remounted and gone on our way, I could not put the thought of them out of my mind. For one thing, both looked careworn, their faces lined and leathery in the bright

morning. But it was the words of the Holy Office that made my heart heavy. If I did not manage to satisfy their request, what would happen to Lucien and Gemma and my cousins? Their very lives were in jeopardy because of me.

It was a long journey to the great city of Paris; I lost count of the days. At the first inn at which we stayed, I took advantage of the night candle to warm the sealing wax and reseal the Inquisitor's letter. It was possible that one of my sleeping companions worked for the Holy Office and would be checking my pack during the night, to see if the packet remained unopened. God help me, were Thomas of York to be handed an unsealed letter!

The landlord, knowing we were poor, did not charge us for the lodging and asked only a few pennies for our supper. The weather remained favorable, and we were able to cover about ten leagues a day. With luck, we'd be in Paris in ten days. Stopping at farms along the way for food and rest helped keep our purses from thinning. The sight of our Dominican robes was enough to make most folk share their simple fare generously. Whenever possible, of course, we stayed at a monastery or a convent, as their hostels were open to all wayfarers.

Finally we came in sight of the roofs of Paris. We had all heard of its splendor, and indeed, it was a great city with a beautiful palace and fine buildings. But the streets were narrow, full of muck and garbage, and crowded with people walking, on horseback, or being carried in sedan

chairs. And the noise! Sellers bellowing their wares, drunks quarreling and bawling as they reeled out of taverns, and minstrels singing and banging their drums as they performed for pennies. Entrancing, perhaps, for some, but I was glad to be trotting out of the city on my horse, headed for Calais. There I gave my sweet mare a kiss on the nose, sad to leave her with the brothers at the monastery.

The next morning, I stood among a group of passengers on the forecastle of a small wooden ship whose prow pointed to the north. There I had my first view of the rippling sea, sun-dappled and magnificent. Waves slapped against the side of the ship in a steady rhythm, and a cool breeze blowing from the English Channel brought the aroma of salt to my nostrils. On the distant horizon was a faint smudge that an excited passenger pointed to: "See? The cliffs of Dover!"

There lay England. I had never seen the shores of a foreign land before.

And Oxford, where I'd have the chance to serve my order in a more exciting way than I'd ever dreamed. It was hard not to feel proud about the importance of my mission. I drew myself up.

Imagine, I was going to be a spy for the Holy Office!

CHAPTER THREE

Only hours out of Calais, the storm struck. It turned the sea into a boiling stew, and we were bits of meat churning about in it. I was sure I would never live to set foot on the shores of England.

The ship that had appeared so sturdy when I boarded was now shuddering and careening at the mercy of the shrieking winds. Worst of all was my feeling of utter helplessness, just waiting for the elements to tear us to pieces. Passengers and crew, we were all about to founder. If only there was something I could do to help!

Dread made my limbs heavy as tree trunks. Was I a

coward, too, as well as a sinner? All about me, the huddled group of passengers moaned and prayed. Faces were gray and eyes wild. I gripped the railing and stared with disbelief toward the western horizon. What had been clear blue sky only moments before was now a mass of scudding black clouds that blotted out the line between sky and water.

A shout made me turn to see the ship's master tearing from place to place on the deck, screaming orders and curses at his men. "Reef the mains'l! Batten down that loose cargo!" He cuffed the face of one young sailor who stood paralyzed with fright. "Lively now, Will!" He shoved him in the direction of the ship's stern. "Help Jack keep 'er headed into the wind!" The sailor set his lips and ran to the helmsman's side. The two pushed with all their strength against the heavy oar fastened to the rudder.

It was hard for me to stand idly by while others were working with all their might. But all I could do was send up prayers to Saint Christopher over and over. A blinding streak of blue lightning split the clouds, followed by a crash of thunder that shook the ship's timbers. The troughs of the waves deepened, and the roll of the ship increased. The first cold drops of rain struck my upturned face like icy stones. I hunched the hood of my robe over my head and prayed with all my soul.

Now the wind gusted to a new fury. Great sprays of water broke over passengers and crew alike. With a

sudden, ear-splitting crack, the top crossbar broke away from the mast and plunged down onto the hapless sailors pulling on the ropes. Screams went up from some of the passengers. Would we all be thrown into the sea next?

"Keep 'er into the wind!" shouted the master to the helmsman. "Don't let 'er get broadside!" He ran toward the tangle of canvas, rope, and men. "Belay the spar! Get the mains'l furled! On your feet, damn yer eyes!"

One sailor lay on deck, writhing and moaning in pain. I leapt the short distance from the forecastle to the deck and ran to his side. Just then, a wall of foaming water cascaded over us. I lost my footing and crashed down onto the deck. Somehow I managed to keep hold of the injured man with one hand and dig the fingernails of the other into a crack between the wooden planks. But the deck, scoured by rain and seawater, was slippery. There was a roaring in my ears and a taste of salt in my mouth. I felt myself sliding toward the side, the rough planks tearing at the flesh of my fingers. The sailor and I were headed for the sea.

Something clamped onto my robe. Turning my head, I saw it was a muscular arm. My sliding slowed, then stopped. I was looking up into the face of a bearded man. As the ship lurched the other way, I managed to scramble to my knees, one hand still clutching the wounded sailor's shirt.

"Hey, lad, up you go!" The strong arm pulled me to my feet. "Now, wait for the next roll of the ship. All right, let's lift him up. But watch out for his right arm, looks broken to me. Now we'll put him down gently."

Together the bearded man and I placed the sailor in a somewhat shielded spot behind the forecastle. He was moaning. The stranger flattened his back against the cabin wall and motioned for me to do the same.

Like an answer to our prayers, the wind and rain began to slacken. The waves settled down to a steady chop. Still growling their anger, the black clouds rolled off toward the east. A line of blue edged the western horizon.

Shouts of glee went up from the sailors. I pulled the wet hood back from my head and faced the man who had saved me. He was a Franciscan—he wore the robe of the Gray Friars. A tonsure of dark hair topped a ruddy face and a broad-shouldered figure. Probably twice my age—about thirty. "Thank you, Brother—if it hadn't been for you—"

"Nonsense, young brother, it was you who risked your neck. You kept that sailor from being washed overboard!"

"My thanks to you both!" The ship's master was approaching the forecastle. "Harry owes his life to you, no mistake." He turned to the passengers. "We've had a bit of bad luck, but there's nothing to worry about. We can make land with just the mains'l. One difference, though—" He paused and glanced at the disk of the sun now visible through the thinning overcast. "We'll have to put in at Portsmouth."

"Portsmouth?" cried a stout merchant. "Look here,

I paid for our passage to London! I insist—"

"You can insist till you're blue in the face! Maybe you've heard of the Cinque Ports pirates, mister? Sail right into their hands, heading for Dover from here. The wind's blown us off course, y'see. So it's either Portsmouth and home safe, or Dover and food for the fishes. Your choice. And besides, mister—" He nodded toward the merchant's wife. "I hear them Dover pirates are right partial to lovely ladies."

The merchant gulped and waved his hand. "Portsmouth it is."

"Well, young pilgrim." The bearded friar smiled at me. "Does this change your plans, too? Where are you going?"

"I'm not on a pilgrimage, Brother. I'm Jean of Toulouse, bound for Oxford. The university."

"Oxford? That's where I'm going! Let me introduce myself—I'm Pierre de Maricourt." We shook hands. "Look here, why don't we travel together?"

"Tell me, where is Portsmouth? Is it far from Oxford? I didn't get much money for travel."

"No problem, young scholar, you'll travel as my guest."

"Your guest?" Who was this man?

As if in answer to my thoughts, he said, "We'll have plenty of time to get acquainted. You must be looking forward to student life."

"Oh, yes. But—"

"But what?"

I hesitated. I couldn't let this stranger know that I dreaded what lay ahead. Instead I said, "Well, they say that at the University of Paris, the best scholars are the Italians. What about Oxford? Can I measure up to them? A Frenchman from a small school like Toulouse?"

The Franciscan threw back his head in laughter. "Italians the best? Why, in Italy, they probably say the French are the best! Rumors like this fly everywhere! Don't believe a word of it."

It was hard not to join in his laughter. Pierre de Maricourt had a way about him. "It's gracious of you to suggest that we travel together."

"Well, then, we'll talk no more about it. The matter is settled. From Portsmouth we'll head for London, and from there to Oxford." Pierre's face grew serious. "Tell me, young friar, do you carry anything for protection?"

I pushed my robe aside to show the dagger in its sheath. "This and the eye of God."

"Good!" Pierre seized my hand. "You're just the man-at-arms I need. So it's settled. Let's find ourselves horses as soon as we go ashore."

Meeting this Franciscan was a godsend. The sparsely filled purse they had given me at the abbey for any expenses outside of university fees would soon have been emptied by this change of plans.

Before I had time even to thank my Franciscan savior, a loud call came from the ship's bow, "L-a-a-nd ho!"

CHAPTER FOUR

Look, we're coming to London Bridge." Pierre reined in his horse. "No wonder the Britons boast."

"It's awesome!" Just seeing it made my heart beat faster. The span against the gray sky was spectacular, even under the light mist that was falling. Two towers guarded each side, with a drawbridge in the center. Along the bridge on both sides, shops were crammed tightly together—clothiers, goldsmiths, grocers, cookshops, apothecaries, and a number of taverns.

Crowds of people were swarming on and off the bridge continuously, pushing and jostling. Pierre leaned over and

touched my arm. "There's such a mob here. Let's get down and lead our horses, or we'll never get through."

I dismounted and took the halter, and Pierre did the same. Even so, we couldn't move very fast. The narrow, cobbled streets were packed with people and horses, carts and carriages. Walking wasn't exactly easy, either, with the filth underfoot.

"Listen." Pierre waggled his eyebrows. "This section near the Thames River is a thief's paradise! Better hang on tight to your purse."

"London's no better than Paris. How can people live so crowded together!" I thrust one hand inside my robe to finger the small leather purse that held the coins that were my whole fortune. Glancing toward Pierre's belt, I was startled to see a bony hand moving toward it slowly and purposefully.

In a flash, I seized the thieving hand, giving it a fearful wrench just as it touched Pierre's belt. "Thief! Thief! I've got him!" A bellow of pain came from the hand's owner, a peddler with a pack of wares on his back, who had squeezed close to us.

"Who? Where is he?" Pierre shouted, looking wildly about.

"His hand was at your purse!" But the peddler had torn himself from my grasp and crashed away through the crowd. The mob had swallowed him up. "I had him! I had him!"

"Calm down, Brother." Pierre touched my shoulder.

"He's gone, and he didn't get a penny. By my oath, you gave him a fright!"

I fingered the pommel of my dagger. "Yes, and if the crowd hadn't pushed him out of my grip, I would have given him a thief's punishment!"

"What a bloodthirsty friar! Come now, punishment is a judge's business. Ours is to forgive."

His words gave me pause; they made me feel hotheaded and heedless. But the thief had roused my anger. "We have a right to defend ourselves, just the same—"

My words died away as I stopped to stare. Just ahead of us was a sight I'd never seen in Toulouse. In front of the shops, fixed point up in the street, stood a number of soldier's pikes. Stuck on two of the sharp points were human heads. They were loose-skinned and decaying. People all around me were passing by without even a glance. I felt my stomach lurch.

Pierre followed my glance. "Oh, the heads. Not much of a welcome to London, is it? Well, they tell me that's how King Henry deals with those who cross him. There's been a bit of a tussle between the king and some of the lesser nobles. When the king gets upset enough to label some of them traitors, why, heads are bound to roll! Sticking them on pikes is just his way of reminding his subjects who really has power. Not exactly delicate, though." He squinted at me. "Are you all right, lad?"

"Of course." But my stomach was still churning. The heads were ghastly. These English were barbarians, to

be sure. What was I doing here, with only a stranger for company? Suddenly I wished I was back in the abbey, even at my least favorite task, sweeping out the barns, listening to the quiet stirrings of the animals. I wouldn't even have minded the smell of dung.

I turned my face in a different direction. "Where are we bound, Brother Pierre?"

"To a nearby inn to spend the night. In the morning we'll get an early start for Oxford. Don't worry, you'll be my guest."

But I did worry. "Why are you being so generous?"

"You risked your neck to save a stranger. Doesn't happen often these days." Pierre grinned. "Besides, we're fellow scholars, aren't we?"

He led the way into a narrow side street that was far less crowded. "Let's remount here." He pulled on his horse's reins. "It's not far, but this mist is turning into rain and the walking will be pretty mucky." We both mounted and rode on.

"But how will I ever repay you?"

Pierre's forehead wrinkled. "I hired you to guard me and you did. You saved my purse! So let's have no more of that." He pointed. "Look, we've arrived. I told you it wasn't far."

The inn was quite different from the usual simple shelter managed by a few monks. We were facing a two-story building of gray stone surrounded by a high brick wall. We trotted through the gateway, and a groom came out

to see to our horses.

As we dismounted, a round, mustached face peered from the front door. Watchful eyes blinked for a moment, then a short, fat figure leaped out and dashed across the courtyard. *"Maître* Pierre, it's you!" He spoke in French, and I was pleased to hear my native language in this barbarian land.

"Louis, my friend!" The two embraced.

The innkeeper drew back. "Oh, a thousand pardons! I'm soiling your coat with my dirty apron."

Pierre laughed. "Come on, Louis, no alchemist is afraid of a dirty apron. It's our trademark."

Alchemist! I had heard plenty of stories about alchemists. They spent their lives bent over scorching furnaces, searching for the magic formula to change lead into gold. It was whispered that in their hidden laboratories, imps and demons were conjured up to help them in their quest. Weren't alchemists in league with the Devil himself?

And Brother Pierre was certainly not like any friar I had ever known. Perhaps that was why I didn't fully trust him in spite of his charm. Without meaning to, I found myself edging away from the Gray Friar.

Meanwhile, Pierre was introducing me. "Louis, this young friar is one of our own countrymen, Jean of Toulouse. Jean, this is the finest host who ever strayed from our cultured land to these barbaric shores—meet Louis Griller."

The innkeeper shook my hand and then glanced upward. "What am I thinking of, keeping you two standing here in the rain! You must be weary, and it's time for supper—come."

We soon found ourselves seated at a table in a big, smoky room. Joints of meat were sizzling on a spit in a wide stone fireplace. The tables were nearly filled with other travelers, mostly men, busy tearing hunks of bread from loaves and swilling drink from goblets. The room throbbed with loud talk, the scraping of benches on the floor, and yells of, "Over 'ere, fill 'er up again, girlie!" to the aproned serving girls. It was steamy and hot, but the aroma of roasting meat made my mouth water.

"Here we are, gentlemen, swimming in its juice, done to a turn!" Louis placed before us a wooden trencher on which sat a tempting joint of beef. One serving girl brought a golden loaf of bread, and the other set down brimming goblets. "Good French wine, not that English vinegar," the innkeeper boasted. He stood beaming while Pierre pulled out his knife and cut a chunk of meat, which he sampled and washed down with a swig of wine.

It was Pierre's turn to beam. "Ah, Louis, living on English soil hasn't spoiled your touch. What flavor—magnificent!"

Louis grinned with satisfaction as he urged us to eat our fill before he hurried off. Pierre was right—both food and drink were of the finest. At our abbey, such a roast would have fed our whole dormitory. The abbot always

warned us against the sin of gluttony. Our meals there were simple, and wine was served only in very modest amounts. So I always ate plenty of bread, which was warm and wholesome, so as not to be a glutton with the meat.

"Come on, eat up, Brother Jean," Pierre urged. "We've got to put some flesh on those bones of yours!"

Did Franciscans not care about the sin of gluttony, then? But my stomach was so empty! It was our first real meal on the journey, I told myself, cutting some more chunks of rare roast beef. And it would be a sin to leave it to be thrown to the growling dogs in the courtyard. Waste was a sin, too. Anyway, there'd be little money at Oxford to splurge on. And here was a feast set before me. It would be foolish not to enjoy it.

Meanwhile, the innkeeper's wife, Marie, came bustling over to the table with him, and the two sat down. Pink-cheeked and cheerful, she towered over her husband. The two Grillers conversed rapidly with Pierre, leaving nothing for me to do but stuff myself. It was easier for me to commit the sin of gluttony than I had thought.

After the feast, Marie led the way to our room. We followed the flickering light of her candlestick up a narrow, wooden staircase to a room with casements overlooking the front courtyard. She set the candle atop a small chest and patted the bed. "It's the very best goose down in that mattress, I saw to it myself! Sleep well, friends."

All too soon, Pierre was shaking me and saying it was high time to get started. When the city gate was opened at dawn, the air was still gloomy and misty, but we had plenty of company. Rich merchants were being carried in horse-drawn litters, while peasants were bumping along in rude ox-carts. Clerics like us were riding horses or asses, and beggars were walking or hobbling with the aid of sticks and crutches. I was glad to be on horseback.

Our ride was uneventful until a strange-looking group approached on foot, noisy and rollicking. Dressed in a motley manner, from monk's robes to threadbare tunics, they cavorted and yelled out jokes to each other. Suddenly Pierre and I were forced to rein in our mounts, for a circle of them surrounded us, prancing around and singing, loudly and off-key:

> Now the holidays are here,
> Close your notebooks without fear;
> Other things will take their place, so
> Down with Latin poems by Naso!

One of them, a skinny figure with matted hair, danced close to us. "Do my eyes deceive me? Can this be our old playmate-in-arms, Pierre? What a sober-face you've become! Look at you, riding like the pope himself! And with a servant in attendance, too! Come on, give your old mates a handout!"

The dance became more frenzied, the shrieks louder.

"Give your old mates a handout! Let's see some silver, some silver!"

I stared at Pierre. "Who are these people?"

Pierre's face was set. "A pack of idiots!" He dug into his purse and flung some coins at the dancers. They scrambled to pick them up, then cheered and opened the circle for us to canter away.

"But they knew your name."

"They're goliards—wandering scholars. Some scholars! I was once like them, a long time ago."

"You were?" This Gray Friar was full of surprises. "What was it like? How old were you then?"

"Just out of the university. Thought I was a man of the world!"

"What did you learn from them?"

"Learn?" He gave a scornful laugh. "How to drink and frolic with women. How to swear like a soldier. How to muck up my life!"

"But they seemed so free and easy."

"Free? Free to starve or steal, you mean. Flouting authority to no purpose!"

Flouting authority? Why was this Gray Friar still wandering about instead of being in an abbey or university? I was silent for a moment. "Obedience is our most important vow, our abbot used to say." As soon as the words left my lips, I thought about the letter hidden in my pack. In one way, being a spy for my order sounded mysterious and thrilling. But at the same time, wasn't there something shameful about being an informer?

And then there was the fact that the Grand Inquisitor had found me guilty, even though I was innocent. What if he was also misinformed about Roger Bacon? What if I couldn't find any proof that Bacon practiced black magic? Would the Holy Office treat Bacon as they had treated me, guilty or not? Did I have to report what they wanted to hear, whether it was true or not?

"Isn't there ever a time, Pierre," I asked, "when blind obedience might be wrong?"

"Ah, that's altogether different," Pierre nodded. "That takes courage. Remember, Socrates refused to be obedient to the citizens of ancient Athens. So they made him drink the poison hemlock that killed him. But people have honored him ever since."

What if I disobeyed the Grand Inquisitor? Would I have the courage to risk my life for the truth? Suddenly I wished with all my heart that I could unburden myself to this man. But I didn't dare trust him.

The day seemed endless. Too many hours in the saddle were making my backside increasingly raw and tender. The mist of the past two days had given way to sunshine which, though welcome at first, was now burning our faces. Just as the red disk of the sun struck the western horizon at our backs, we trotted up a little rise in the road. Pierre reined in his horse and pointed. "Look!"

Far off, against the darkening sky, I could make out

spires rising above a stretch of trees.

"Oxford!" shouted the alchemist. "We're here!"

I sucked in my breath. For so long, I had dreamed of going to a university. But not this university. Not even this country.

And not with a letter from the Holy Office in my pack.

CHAPTER FIVE

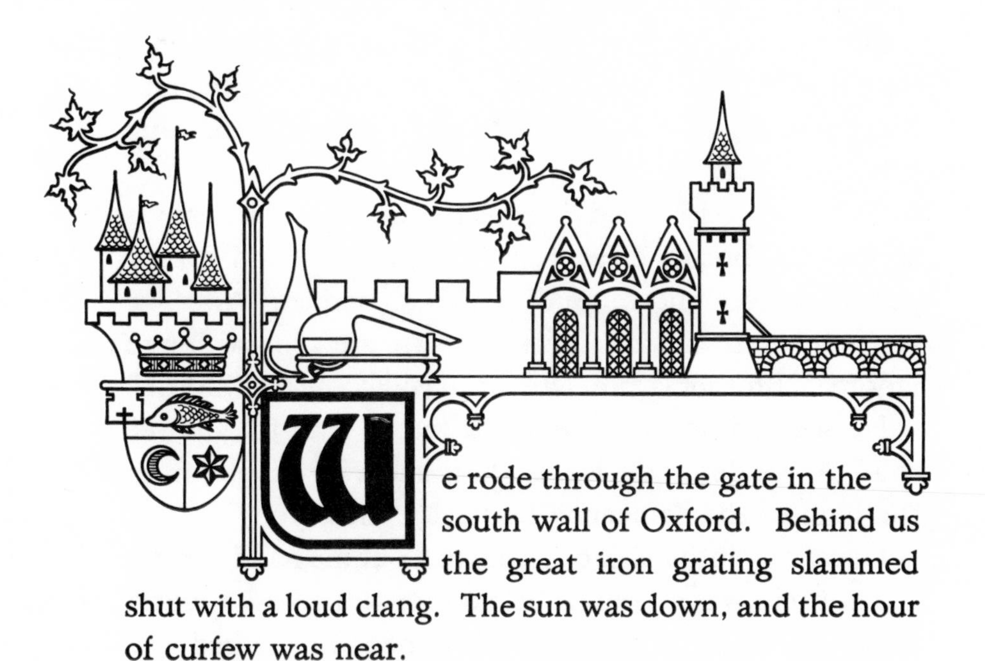

We rode through the gate in the south wall of Oxford. Behind us the great iron grating slammed shut with a loud clang. The sun was down, and the hour of curfew was near.

I dismounted and handed the reins to Pierre. "What's this?" he asked.

"Brother Pierre, you have been too generous. I can't thank you enough. But we're in Oxford now, and I can take care of myself."

"Where will you go?"

"Why, to Saint Edmund Hall at the university. That's

where I'm supposed to report."

"At this hour? Nonsense, the university gates are locked fast. And don't forget the curfew. If the guard picks you up, you'll spend the night in jail. Besides, I'm still in debt to you for saving my purse in London. So you're my guest for one more night—and no arguments."

How would I ever repay this man? But it had been a long ride in mostly poor weather, and I was too tired and hungry to argue. "Maybe someday I can do something for you."

So my horse followed Pierre's to a small inn, where we supped on bread, dried fish, and ale. I found myself puzzling more and more over this alchemist. After we were shown to our room, my curiosity grew too strong to ignore. "Brother Pierre, why have you come to Oxford?"

He seemed not to have heard me. "Wait till you see this! A wonderful device, given to me by a traveler from the land of the Saracens. Look, I'll show you."

Pierre dug into his pack and stuck out his hand. In his palm, there was a long, thin piece of stone and a round cork. He went to the crude table next to the bed and poured some water from the pitcher into the washing bowl. Then he floated the cork on the water. This was no magic—everyone knew that cork floated on water.

But then he carefully laid the length of stone on the cork. To my amazement, the cork began to twist in the water. Finally, it stopped.

"What is it?" I asked.

"This, my young friar, is called the lodestone. It possesses a power known as magnetism. Notice which way the ends are pointing. Now I give it a whirl—"

Again, after turning about, the two ends of the stone pointed in the same directions as before! Pierre spun the lodestone again, and once more it came back to its original position. I could scarcely believe my eyes.

"It doesn't change!"

"That's right! This floating sliver of stone will always point north and south. It's said that the merchants of Cathay—"

"Cathay? Then there is such a land?"

"Oh, yes—far, far to the east. They say merchants there use lodestones to guide their ships."

It was fascinating to see that little piece of rock point unswervingly in the same direction. But at the same time, I couldn't help feeling uneasy. Alchemy, black magic, the lodestone—it all kept churning in my brain. "Why did you bring it to Oxford?"

Pierre smiled. "To show it to an old friend—Roger Bacon. He's a brilliant philosopher and a great teacher. Wait till you attend one of his lectures!"

Bacon! The very heretic I was supposed to catch for the Holy Office! Was this Franciscan who had befriended me his accomplice? So all my suspicions were true. Brother Pierre was a henchman of Satan, too.

He was yawning. "Well, enough experimenting for tonight. My bones are weary, and yours must be, too.

Let's get to sleep."

Again I lay awake in the dark, thinking about how God had directed my path. Was Pierre's magic a sign that the Grand Inquisitor was right after all? And I was sharing a bed with this dangerous man. I whispered a prayer to myself and made the sign of the cross. Finally, the soft nickering of the horses in the stable below and the muted footsteps of the guard marching through the streets nearby lulled me to sleep.

Pierre was snoring softly when I awoke. It was barely light, but a cart was already rumbling through the courtyard. I eased myself out of bed, dressed quickly, and left the room on tiptoe. Not the best way to reward his kindness, perhaps. But the whole puzzle of the Franciscan, between his practice of alchemy and the magic of the lodestone, made me feel more and more uncomfortable about him. The truth was that I found myself drawn to him but still dared not trust him.

Out in the street, I stopped a short man wearing a cobbler's apron. I had learned English from several visiting brothers who had stayed at the abbey in Toulouse for some time, but when I asked this man how to get to the university, he answered me with only a frown and a shrug before he hurried away. Puzzled, I asked the same question of a second, a uniformed guard, who gave me a sour look but told me how to get there. Did everyone in England dislike friars, or was it my French accent? Finally I came to the great open gate in the wall surrounding Oxford

University and entered.

Little clusters of people dotted the spacious quadrangle between the halls of the university. I walked between them, clutching my pack and trying not to show my excitement. Older students were greeting each other with loud cries and mutual slaps on the back. Faculty professors, recognizable by their long black gowns, strode by. The early morning sun was lighting up a noisy, busy scene.

I looked about, hoping to find another newcomer like myself. Ahead of me, a student about my own age was standing apart and staring about him with an expression of bewilderment. I walked up to him. "Hello, are you a first-year student, too?"

"Does it show?" He grinned. "I'm Giles—Giles Rowley from London." Curly brown hair topped brown eyes in a square-jawed face. His figure was a bit heavier than mine.

"Jean of Toulouse." We shook hands. I noted that Giles had neither a friar's robe nor a friar's shaven pate. "You're not a member of an order?"

"No, I'm not." He grinned again. "But they do let some of us in."

"Where are you assigned?"

"Saint Edmund Hall, of course. That's the Southern Nation."

"Southern Nation? Oh, isn't that the part of the university for foreigners?"

"Right. And for Englishmen, too. The Northerners are

the Irish and the Scots. I hear they're barbarians, ready to tear you apart at the drop of a hat."

I parted my robe to show the pommel of my dagger. "I can take care of myself."

"Me, too." Giles did the same.

"Do you know where the hall is?"

"Someone pointed it out to me. Come on, we'll go together."

Saint Edmund's turned out to be a long building of gray stone with a sloping, tiled roof. We walked through the open doors into a huge hall. The ceiling seemed to be almost as high as heaven itself. Flags of many crests hung on the paneled walls.

Giles and I joined a group of students who were standing before a desk where the master of the hall sat, garbed in a professor's robe and flat-topped hat. Before him was a large open book in which he scribbled as each student answered his questions. While we waited, Giles and I told each other about ourselves. His father was a well-to-do cloth merchant in London who was sending Giles to Oxford to study mathematics. Someday Giles would take over the business and be responsible for keeping the accounts.

"Well, are you two here to register or to chatter away like magpies?" The sarcastic voice of the master broke in on our conversation.

"Oh, sorry, sir." Giles reddened and stepped before the desk. The master entered his name in the book and

told him where he was to be quartered. Giles paid his fee and moved to one side to wait for me.

"Jean of Toulouse, eh? Ah, yes, I have a note here about you. We don't get many scholarship students from France. Hmm, let's see: Dominican order, all fees paid for the first two years. Following payments dependent on performance as a scholar." He bent over the book, muttering to himself as he wrote, "...of Toulouse, candidate for the Baccalaureate...this day, thirteenth of August...Year of Our Lord, 1264...quartered in..." He looked up at me. "Room number 40 on the second floor, northwest corner. Be here tomorrow after breakfast for the taking of oaths."

I thanked him and made way for the next in line.

Giles's face was wreathed in a smile. "Number 40? Great, we're sharing a room!"

The room turned out to be stuffy and dark. Still, it was large enough to hold two coarse pallets stuffed with straw. It grew lighter when we opened the shutters of a high window on the north side, letting in the freshness of the summer morning. There was a rough woolen blanket on each bed, a washstand with a pitcher and basin, and on the wall, a shelf for books and writing materials, and pegs to hang garments.

"Ugh!" Giles snorted. "It's a dungeon! Not even any glass in the window. It'll rain right in on us!"

I laughed. "Dungeon? You should see our dormitory at the abbey in Toulouse—hardly room enough to turn

yourself around. And mice and spiders for company. *That's* a dungeon. This room is a palace!"

Giles shrugged. "No use griping, I'll just have to get used to it. Anyway, my father is sending up a chest of clothing. You can store your things in it, too."

"Thanks. Mine won't take up much space." I tossed my pack on one of the beds. "Well, what'll we do now?"

Giles flung his things on the other. "Nothing to do till tomorrow..." His face brightened. "How about exploring the place?"

"Good thinking! Here's our chance to see the town!"

We walked across the grassy quadrangle and out the college gate into the crowded streets of Oxford. Shopkeepers were setting up stands outdoors, putting out their wares for the flood of students. Room-for-rent signs were posted on the doors of houses. From the many taverns came smells of roasting meat, and shouts and scraps of song from revelers.

At one corner, my elbow grazed the arm of a woman moving past with a large market basket on her head. "Madam, a thousand pardons."

She stopped to shift her load back into balance again and scowled at me. "Student scum!" she snarled and spat on the pavement at my feet.

"Well!" Giles stared at me. "They told me to expect no love between the townspeople and the students. But I didn't know it was this bad."

My taste for sight-seeing was gone. "Let's go back to

the university."

"But we haven't seen anything yet," protested Giles. He saw that I was determined. "All right, but first let me stake you to some refreshments. That smell of roast meat is driving me mad."

We found a tavern on a side street that seemed quiet; about half a dozen men were already drinking as we walked in. Next to the fireplace were two large wooden barrels set on their sides, with spigots. Light from the long window showed a floor that needed sweeping.

We chose a table and sat. A sullen girl in a grimy dress came to take our order. "Wine," said Giles, trying to sound grown-up and experienced. "And what's that meat on the spit?"

"Pork. Farthing a portion." She tossed her head.

"Two portions, then, and well roasted, mind you."

She sniffed and went off to fetch the order.

We had hardly begun to attack the chunks of meat with our knives when a loud voice rose above the murmurs of conversation. "Och, man, d'ye call this vinegared swill wine?"

A giant figure with a shock of flaming red hair, goblet in hand, had risen from one of the tables and was looming over the red-faced innkeeper.

"Swill? You call that swill? That's the best wine in these parts! You students are always complaining!"

The giant's answer was to take a swig of the wine and spit it in a long, red stream onto the floor. "Vinegar, that's

what it is!"

The innkeeper waved his hands wildly, yelling, "Out! Out! We don't need insults from the likes of you! You call yourself a man, dressed in a skirt?"

"It's no skirt, you ignoramus, it's a kilt! Now gi' me back the farthing ye stole from me!"

"Them that drinks, pays!" With a scream of rage, the innkeeper ran back to the fireplace, grabbed a thick iron stirring rod, and came back to threaten the tall complainer. "Out! Or I'll bash your bloody head in!"

The giant's answer was to toss the goblet at the innkeeper, staining his shirt and apron red. Next, he raised his foot and sent the innkeeper sprawling.

"Help! Help!" bawled the fallen man. "All townsmen, help!"

As one, the other men at the tables leaped to their feet and rushed to the innkeeper's side with knives clenched in their fists. Slowly and menacingly, the entire group moved toward the giant. Giles and I could only stare in amazement.

"So it's six against one, is it?" The giant pulled a long sword from the scabbard in his belt. His glance flickered our way. "Be ye scholars, lads? To my side, then!"

I looked at Giles, who read the question in my face. He set his lips and jumped up. "Let's go!" We had just taken out our knives in anticipation of the meat Giles had ordered. A moment later, we stood by the giant's side. My heart began to beat faster. In spite of all the bravado

I had shown Pierre in London, I had never actually fought for my life before.

"Welcome, lads!" roared the student, whose shoulders loomed a good six inches above mine. "Two of them for each of us—that evens the score!"

Suddenly six more townsmen, led by the waitress, appeared at the tavern door. They were armed with pikes and staves, and one held a pitchfork with long, rusted tines. "There's them stinkin' scholars!" the girl screamed. "Get 'em!"

"Och!" muttered the giant. "Looks like the odds have changed, lads. Follow me when I give ye the word."

He took a step forward and pointed to the doorway. "Look out! The guard! Over there!" As the townsmen all turned to see, he whispered, "Now!" and leapt for the wall where the great casks stood. With quick twists he opened the taps, flooding the floor with ale and wine. He pulled away the wooden bar from a small back door behind the casks. By the time the innkeeper and his army realized they'd been tricked, we were bolting through the door and dashing down the alleyway.

Out in the street, we pushed ourselves into the middle of the crowd that had gathered to see what was going on. We could hear alarms being raised, and somewhere a church bell began to toll in short, angry clangs.

"There they go! After 'em! Don't let 'em get away!"

"Och, lads, they're on to us! Let's make for the university gates, no time to dally!" Our new redheaded friend

ran in long easy strides. We two barely managed to keep up with him.

Once, I twisted my head to look behind. A motley mob of armed men was gaining on us. "Faster, fellows!" I panted. "They're on our heels!"

Our speed increased as though we wore the winged sandals of Mercury, the messenger of the gods. The angry townsmen were only a few yards behind us when the university gates came into view. We hurled ourselves through them, turned around, and shouted "Sanctuary! Sanctuary!" with our last bit of breath.

The mob, snarling and shaking their fists and weapons, stood there and screamed insults. But they did not dare invade Church territory—they knew the penalties too well. After a few minutes, they dispersed, still vowing vengeance on us.

We flung ourselves down on the grass, laughing and enjoying our escape. I didn't want to think about what would have happened if they'd caught us.

"Och, lads, 'tis lucky for me you were in the tavern when the ruckus started." Our new friend raised himself on one elbow and held out his hand. "Ian MacIver's the name. From the North Country." We shook hands and introduced ourselves. "I'd never refuse the hand of a man just because he's from the Southern Nation. Never have held with the notion that you're all namby-pamby idiots."

"Do all Scots dress like that?" I'd never seen a man in a kilt before.

"This plaid is my family tartan—the clan colors. The MacIvers have worn it for five generations. We're a hot-tempered lot, I'm afraid—always brawling and no help for it."

"Why? Is it clan against clan?"

"Sometimes, but mostly it's us against the English. We'd like to get out from under the king's yoke." Ian scrambled to his feet. "Well, lads, I'm off to my hall. I'll say it again, ye're a good pair. It's my treat to a tankard of ale next time we meet." He waved at us and trotted off.

Giles looked at me. "When I write home to my father, should I mention this affair?"

I started to laugh. "Tell him we were greeted by the Oxford welcoming committee!"

CHAPTER SIX

Our first real day at Oxford began with the taking of oaths. After the hour of prime and a hasty breakfast of porridge in the hall's dining room, Giles and I joined the other new students in the great front room. Before us on a raised platform stood the master of St. Edmund's with a large Bible on the table next to him.

"Attention!" called the master. "Silence! All raise your right hands. You will now swear on the Holy Book that you will adhere to the following behaviors. Repeat after me: I swear that I will respect and obey all commands or requests given by the master of St. Edmund's."

We repeated the oath in unison.

There followed a long list of "I wills" and "I will nots" which we mumbled in repetition after the master. Giles winked at me as we intoned, "I will not seek willful revenge on a master who fails me in a course," and "I will not gamble my money away in taverns, nor will I sell my books for money to spend on wine and women."

After the ceremony, we all left to seek out our tutors. Mine was a Master John Peckham. Outside the hall, I was approached by a man wearing the Dominican colors under his black master's robe, eyeing me sharply. "You are Jean of Toulouse?" He was a commanding figure, white-haired around his pate and white-bearded, with a ruddy complexion.

"Yes?"

His lips widened in a smile. "Welcome to Oxford, Brother Jean." His hand clapped my shoulder. "I'm Thomas of York. It's good to see another Dominican robe in this hotbed of Franciscans!"

I hadn't expected such a cordial greeting from a representative of the Holy Office. "Thank you—" Was I to call him Brother or Master? I decided the latter would show more respect. "—Master Thomas."

The smile did not leave his face. "You have something for me, do you not?" At the same time, his gray eyes seemed to be studying me.

My spirits fell. In the excitement of my initiation to the university, I had all but forgotten about the Grand

Inquisitor and my mission. So this distinguished-looking man held my fate in his hands. "It's up in my room. Will you wait here, or shall I bring it to your chambers?"

"Bring it here, no use wasting time." His tone was like that of a magistrate.

I dashed upstairs to my room, found the sealed packet, and hurried back with it.

Master Thomas seized the packet, snapped open the seal, and stood reading it. His smile had become a frown. He proceeded to instruct me as to my duties regarding Roger Bacon. "Take care, go about this with extreme caution. We are not dealing with an ordinary human here. This man can invoke charms and spells that can steal your soul!"

I shifted from one foot to the other as I nodded.

Master Thomas put the packet inside his robe. "Now, we will have to find a way to get you close to Bacon. Let me think..." He pursed his lips. "Ah, I have it—there's the very person we need—Bacon's assistant." His voice boomed out. "Brother Johannus! A moment, please!"

A slight figure in a gray Franciscan robe turned and came over to where we were standing. Sandy-colored hair topped blue eyes in a freckled face. He appeared to be a bit older than I. His face had a puzzled, almost wary expression.

"Brother Johannus, meet a new student just arrived from France—Brother Jean of Toulouse. As you can see, we are both Dominicans. Brother Jean tells me he has

heard of the work of Master Bacon and is most intrigued. I wonder if you might be able to spare a little time and take him in hand? You should know that he is here on a full scholarship."

Thomas's hand on my shoulder propelled me toward the assistant. But it was his words that amazed me. Roger Bacon? Intrigued with him? Thomas of York spoke these lies so smoothly, so blandly. Of course, he had known about my coming. But his quick scheming took my breath away. Perhaps lying was a skill that came with the practice of law.

Brother Johannus was shaking my hand. "Brother Jean of Toulouse, welcome! I've already heard good things about you from Pierre de Maricourt."

The silver eyebrows of Thomas of York rose in surprise. "You know the Franciscan Petrus Peregrinus?"

I didn't understand. "Petrus?"

"That's his Latin name," Johannus grinned. "He's always on the go, so we call him the Wandering Rock—a little joke. He told us how you two met on the Channel ship and traveled here together."

"Ah," Thomas nodded. "Well, I must be off. I have a lecture to give. Why don't you come to my rooms after vespers this evening, Brother Jean, and you can give me all the news about my friends in Toulouse." He turned to Johannus. "Then you'll take our young friend in hand, Brother Johannus?" Smiling again, Thomas inclined his head and strode off.

"I'd better go, too." It was a relief to see my fellow Dominican leave. "I'm supposed to find my tutor, Master John Peckham."

"Peckham? He's a good man, you're lucky. Look, it's on my way, I'll walk with you."

We walked quickly. "What sort of work do you do for Master Bacon?"

Johannus's face lit up. "I help with experiments and try to keep the laboratory in order. Oh, he's the most wonderful man! After I finished his courses, he invited me to become his assistant."

To hear Bacon described as "the most wonderful man" surprised me. "What kind of experiments does he do?"

"Are you really interested in discovering the secrets of nature?" He gave me a sideways glance.

Secrets of nature? Was this the black magic of which I had been warned? The idea of engaging in such work was frightening. At the same time, it seemed an exciting challenge. Besides, the instructions of the Holy Office were clear. "Yes, I am. Especially after Brother Pierre showed me the lodestone."

"He showed you that?" It was his turn to be surprised. "Then he does think highly of you." He was quiet for a moment. "The fact is, most students are reluctant to work in the laboratory. But we need extra hands. Do you want to join us? You'll earn a bit, too."

What went on in that laboratory that made other students afraid of it? My heart beat faster, but I answered

firmly, "Yes, I do want to work with you."

Johannus told me where the laboratory was and said I could find him there any time during the day. Finally I was free to dash off to meet my tutor.

Master John Peckham was mild-mannered and pleasant but quick to get to the heart of my interests. "So it's mathematics in the quadrivium that interests you the most, Brother Jean." The quadrivium part of the curriculum contained, in addition to arithmetic and geometry, courses in astronomy and music. "Good. We have some fine mathematicians on the faculty here. Remember what Plato wrote at the entrance to his school, the Academy?"

"Let no one enter who does not know geometry!" I had learned that only this past year.

"Excellent. Well, I can see that we'll get along. I accept you as my student. Please sign your name in my book. Lectures will begin after prime tomorrow in St. Edmund's."

Right where Giles and I lived—what luck! I took the quill pen and wrote. "Sir, may I ask a question?"

"Of course."

"I have been asked to be a helper in Master Roger Bacon's laboratory. If I accept that offer, will it interfere with my studies?"

"Bacon's laboratory?" His brow furrowed. "Doesn't attract many here." Then he smiled. "Why not? Master Bacon's a great believer in the power of mathematics.

Might actually be good for you. I have no objection. But—" He paused.

"Sir?"

He stroked his chin. "I wouldn't go talking about it, if I were you. Master Bacon doesn't have many friends here. Be careful."

"Thank you, Master Peckham." I left his rooms grateful that God had granted my prayers—I was a university scholar, ready to learn everything there was to know in the world.

But the shadow of Thomas of York hovered over me. And I'd made a bargain with Johannus to work in Bacon's laboratory. It was all settled, there was no backing out now. Oh, Master John Peckham, I'd better be careful, all right.

Was I going to be working for a brilliant scientist?

Or as an apprentice to the Devil?

CHAPTER SEVEN

My steps lagged as I approached New College. Just thinking about the meeting with Master Thomas of York had kept me from savoring my dinner. Sitting next to me at the long table tonight, Giles soon noticed that I wasn't attacking the stew with my usual gusto. The big refectory was noisy with chatter and the clank of knives and spoons, so he had to raise his voice. "Jean, you don't have a thing to worry about! Listen, you clerics are always the top scholars. I'm the one that'll fall behind, wait and see!" But it wasn't the lectures that were preying on my mind.

I stood for a minute staring at Master Thomas's paneled door before I knocked. "Enter!" his loud voice boomed out after a second. I opened the door and walked into a room more luxurious than any I had ever seen, quite different from the plain quarters of Master John Peckham. Late sunlight streaming through the window picked out the brilliant hues of embroidered tapestries on the walls and gleamed on richly carved chairs. Thomas sat behind a polished desk set on a thick rug of Persian design. "Come in, come in!" He gave an impatient wave of his arm. "Here, sit down."

I sat in the chair next to him and tried to appear at ease, wondering what had happened to his vow of poverty. He was a Dominican, after all, a member of my own order.

"Now, tell me what went on between you and Brother Johannus." He leaned back in his chair and stroked the taut skin of his cheek with his knuckles.

"Oh, I've agreed to work in Master Bacon's laboratory. I'm to meet Johannus there tomorrow. It's all arranged."

"Excellent! Excellent!" A look of satisfaction crossed his broad face. "It seems that your meeting with de Maricourt has played into our hands." He rubbed his plump hands together—the hands in which the Holy Office had placed not only my life, but also that of my family. "Your even knowing him was a surprise to me." His tone implied that being chummy with Pierre was itself a sin.

"He actually saved my life during a storm in the English Channel. And then he was kind enough to pay my

expenses from Portsmouth on."

"Ah, you're very young and inexperienced, my friend. There's always a price to be paid for that kind of generosity." Thomas's voice was heavy with irony. "Let us pray the price is not your very soul!" His fingers drummed on the desk. "Now to the business at hand. The way things stand, Bacon considers me an enemy. So I have not been able to learn anything about what he's up to. God knows what unholy works are being carried out under our very noses!" He eyed me. "The sooner you start in the laboratory, the better. And one part of your task is especially pressing."

"What's that?" I leaned forward.

"It's rumored that in Bacon's laboratory there's a head cast in bronze. A gift from *Satan himself.*" His voice had grown hushed to almost a whisper.

"From Satan—" A shiver flickered down my spine. The sun was going down, and the room was darker.

"Further, they say that when Bacon utters certain magical commands, this head speaks and predicts the future!" Thomas moistened his lips and pressed them together.

"How can this—"

"Your task," he interrupted severely, "will be to find out where the head is kept. Then you must be witness to this unnatural act. Just think, it is your evidence that will send Bacon and his crew to the stake! Including Pierre de Maricourt, of course!"

The stake! I sucked in my breath. My words would be responsible for the slaughter of Pierre. And a man I had not even met, Roger Bacon, whom Johannus had called "wonderful." Perhaps even freckle-faced Johannus as well.

A little doubt stirred at the back of my mind. The Church had thought me a heretic, too. I had no idea why. What kind of evidence might they accept to justify killing these three?

Master Thomas leaned forward, his jaw tense. "Remember, Jean of Toulouse. You are to be vigilant every moment. Never forget we are dealing with agents of the Devil." His words were deliberate, dropped like stones. "I will expect to hear from you before long. Come at the same hour, as soon as you have matters to report. Now, is everything clear?"

The room seemed unbearably close. "Perfectly clear, Master Thomas." I got to my feet, mumbled a good night, and hurried from his rooms. Outside, the sun was setting in a splendor of color, and an evening breeze had sprung up. Three students passed me, arguing loudly about Aristotle's rules of logic, and somewhere a bell was tolling. I took a deep breath and exhaled before dashing across the quadrangle to St. Edmund's. Geometry would be simple compared to spying for my fellow Dominican. The burden of three lives lay on my shoulders.

In the morning, Giles came with me to Master Peckham's first mathematics lecture. We found Ian MacIver there, too. To the surprise of the other Southern Nation students in the class, he greeted us warmly. I overheard a whispered, "Who ever heard of a barbarian from the North being friendly to any of us!"

Peckham began with a summary of elementary geometry before plunging into more advanced material that I had trouble following. It was a relief to me after the lecture when both Giles and Ian began to complain.

"Och!" Ian rolled his eyes. "I never saw the likes of that in Inverness! If he keeps that up, lads, I'll be back in Scotland before the leaves turn!"

"You're not the only one, Ian. He lost me halfway through." Giles shook his head and looked at me. "I suppose our scholarship friend here got it all down pat?"

"Very funny, Giles. But never mind, fellows. I'll wager most of the others had just as much trouble as we did. Anyway, we'll study together—three heads are better than one." Then I remembered my appointment with Johannus. "Look, I've got to run."

"Where to, man? Have ye got another lecture this early?"

I shook my head. "No, I'm starting work as an assistant in Master Roger Bacon's laboratory. Have you heard anything about him?"

Ian looked puzzled and just shrugged. But Giles's eyes opened wide. "Bacon? You mean the one who's supposed to be flirting with the Devil? What made you join that strange crew? It'll take a lot of nerve to walk into

that place!"

Ian put his hand on his sword. "D'ye wish me to come along, laddie?"

"No, thanks, Ian. The fact is, I need the money. Just wish me luck." I left the two of them gaping after me.

Master Bacon's laboratory was in a small, ivy-covered building almost hidden by shrubbery in one corner of the quadrangle. As I approached, I noticed that most students were going out of their way to avoid passing close to the doorway. One or two crossed themselves as they hurried by, as did one of the masters in his flapping black gown.

A few students stopped to stare as I stood hesitating on the stoop. All the tales I'd ever heard about the Devil and his fiendishly clever ways came flooding into my mind. What chance would I have, I who could not even follow a geometry lecture! If only I could run back and join Giles and Ian, who were probably enjoying a glass of ale together right now. But the long arm of the Holy Office would find me before long. What was worse, they would find my uncle and aunt. I crossed myself before raising my head high and pushing open the heavy door.

The corridor was dark and reeked of sulfur. A door stood open at the opposite end, and I could make out two figures moving about in the room beyond. One of them came forward and looked out.

"Brother Jean?" It was Johannus, wearing a stained leather apron over his tunic. "Come on in!"

Though it was morning, the windows were shuttered,

and light came from blazing candles placed all around. In one corner, a fire burned fiercely in a furnace made of stone and fire-clay, with a large bellows arranged to blow up the fire. Over the fire sat an oddly shaped ceramic vessel, hissing and emitting a reddish smoke. The room was intensely hot, and the smell of sulfur was overwhelming. A wave of dizziness passed over me from the heat and the odor, followed by a sense of panic that made my right hand grip my left to keep them from shaking.

"Take off your robe—you'll be more comfortable." Johannus exchanged my robe for an apron like his. "Come meet Master Bacon."

Roger Bacon was sitting on a large bench before a table on which stood flasks and jars of different shapes and sizes containing powders and liquids. He was pouring a dark liquid from one flask into another. As he poured, the liquid changed to a bright yellow color. It was the first magic I had seen, except for the lodestone. Was this the work of Satan? Gooseflesh prickled my arms, and I longed to run away. But I had my orders.

"Master, this is Jean of Toulouse. He's going to help us."

"I'll be with you directly." Bacon's gaze stayed on his task. He finished pouring and held up the yellow flask against the candlelight. "Perfect." He set the flask down and turned to me. "So, Jean of Toulouse, my old friend Pierre has spoken to me of you. Welcome to our workplace!"

The mention of Pierre's name made me feel uncomfortable. What had he told Bacon about me? How I'd paid for his kindness by slipping away without a word of farewell?

Meanwhile, Bacon had risen and was shaking my hand. I found myself looking into a striking countenance, one not easily forgotten. A long, hawklike nose, black hair streaked with white, eyes dark and shiny as agates. Like Johannus, he was wearing a much-used apron. But he had the ringing voice and the self-assurance of a king. Was he the King of Darkness?

I found my voice and thanked him. "Well, now," Bacon went on, "you seem to be wearing the proper clothing for this place. Why don't we put him to work, Johannus. Show Jean how to blow up the fire. I need more heat to melt some lead."

Johannus showed me how to work the great bellows. As my arm moved up and down, the coals in the furnace glowed more brightly and began to flame. Bacon placed a small clay pot on the grate. "This is a crucible, Jean, and that"—he motioned to the long-necked vessel—"we call a pelican." He stepped back and looked at the fire. "Good, good! Keep it up!"

While I worked, my eyes scanned the rest of the room. Shelves covered with bottles large and small, twisted tubes of glass like corkscrews, strange-shaped vessels of either clay or metal, and books. Books! I had never seen so many in one place except in the scriptorium of the abbey.

But what was nowhere to be seen in the laboratory was anything resembling a head made of bronze. A head that could foretell the future. At least for the moment, I felt better. I didn't have to deal with a talking head.

CHAPTER EIGHT

My life at Oxford soon came to be divided between two very different worlds. Part of me behaved like a typical Oxford student. I zigzagged from morning Mass to lectures in grammar, rhetoric, logic, and mathematics. Whenever possible, Giles and Ian joined me for evening study sessions that sometimes turned into romps.

The more unbelievable part of my life was spent in Roger Bacon's laboratory. During the first few weeks, Johannus taught me some of the basics of alchemy—the art of discovering how the different kinds of matter in nature can be joined or broken apart to form new kinds.

When I stammered something about my abbot's views on alchemy, Johannus laughed.

"Yes, Jean, you'll find many here, too, who think that we're performing unnatural acts. Don't listen to them. Alchemy is a science. There is much to be learned about what happens to matter when it's roasted or amalgamated."

He began teaching me the names of the different vessels. Then I learned the names of different earths and liquids. And I was fascinated by that most magic of all metals, mercury—the silver that spills like water. Johannus led me through the techniques of distillation, evaporation, and amalgamation.

"Remember," he told me, "fire is the most important agent of change. The furnace of an alchemist must never go out!" That meant I had to make sure a good supply of wood was always next to the large iron furnace.

But what I'd expected to learn did not happen. Master Bacon had no special ways of calling upon the Powers of Darkness for magical transformations. Johannus did not draw any pentagrams or any other of the symbols that went along with getting Satan's attention. In spite of myself, I was drawn to the two men more and more. Almost every day, Master Bacon took the time to explain patiently the meaning of an experiment. And one morning, after he'd finished speaking and turned back to his work, a shiver of discovery prickled all the way up my spine to the very top of my head. Suddenly everything became clear. It wasn't the work of the Devil I was learning

from this man, but the workings of nature itself.

So when I crossed the quadrangle to report to Thomas of York for the first time, I really had nothing to report.

His face darkened. "What? You've been in that cursed laboratory all this time and found nothing? How can that be?"

I shrugged. "Nothing, Master Thomas. They all work hard, that's all."

He got up from his chair and began to pace about the room. "What about the bronze head?"

"No sign of it in the laboratory anywhere. I've looked in every corner and closet."

"Is it possible—" He paused a moment and his eyes narrowed. "Is it possible that they suspect you? That they've hidden it deliberately until they're certain they can trust you?"

"Well," I said weakly, "I don't think so..."

"Well, then." Master Thomas plumped himself back in his chair and drummed the fingers of his right hand on the table. "Let's consider more drastic measures. Master Bacon does have living quarters apart from the laboratory. Perhaps the head is there, for safekeeping."

"But how would I ever—I'd have to be invited—"

"Nonsense," he interrupted, and held up his hand. "Let me think a moment." After a bit, he beckoned me to lean closer. "Find out if he spends any nights at the laboratory. Then you can simply get into his quarters and locate the head. Let me know which night—I'll find a way

for you to get in."

"But Master Thomas—" I was aghast at the idea of breaking into another person's private dwelling, let alone that of Master Bacon. "That's against the law!"

"Law? Come, come, Jean of Toulouse! Fighting heresy is more important than any civil law!"

"But what if I'm caught?"

"You are to do as I say! No task is impossible—don't even consider failure. Remember, the Holy Office is our law!"

How could I argue with him? I muttered that I would try it, and got out of there. All the way back to the dormitory, I fought a mental battle with Brother Thomas against doing what he had commanded. Why had I given in so easily? What a namby-pamby coward I was! In truth, I had now begun to believe that the Holy Office was mistaken. But how could I ever say that to Master Thomas?

Up in my room, I found Ian pacing up and down, and Giles with a long face. "What's wrong?" I asked.

Giles turned to Ian. The Scotsman pounded a fist into the palm of his other hand. "It's no use, Jean, this stuff's not for the likes of me. And I'll never be using all those rules of rhetoric and grammar they're throwing at us. Besides—" He lowered his voice. "—word has come that my father, the Laird of Inverness, is dead."

I tried to find words. "That's terrible, Ian."

Ian shook his great, shaggy head and heaved a sigh.

"It's the Lord's will. Anyway, I have to return and take over my father's duties." He waved away our protestations at losing his friendship. "Och, we'll still be friends, lads, not to worry about that. And if either of you ever has need of my help, send word to Inverness and I'll come running, d'ye hear?" He took my hand. "Especially you, Jean, in that alchemist's nest."

"Thanks, Ian. But I can take care of myself." Brave words; were they true? Losing Ian was a blow. Life at Oxford wouldn't be the same without him.

Giles and I put our hands together with Ian's and pledged eternal friendship. Then we walked Ian to his dormitory and bade him a final farewell. He had decided to leave in the morning.

Giles was lucky—he fell asleep the minute we'd blown out our candles. But I found myself tossing about on my straw pallet. What would become of me if I was caught stealing into Roger Bacon's apartment? Would the Holy Office defend me? Or would they deny all knowledge of my motives and let me rot in some dank English dungeon? Worse still, could my head end up decorating the top of one of those sharp English pikes? Even when sleep overtook me, horrible shapes chased through my dreams.

The morning brought me no relief. I would have to do Thomas's bidding, though I could try to stall for time.

Stalling wasn't easy. Giles assumed I was glum over Ian's leaving, so he didn't question me about my moping. But in the laboratory, where working with my hands was

usually so satisfying, I felt guiltier than ever facing Master Bacon and Johannus. During the past few weeks, I had come to feel certain that the accusations of the Holy Office against Master Bacon were a huge mistake. Nevertheless, I could not refuse to carry out the orders of Master Thomas. Who at the Holy Office would believe me, an accused heretic? It would be my worthless word against that of a well-known professor.

One day, I heard Master Bacon tell Johannus to plan to work late that night. Because I had an early-morning lecture, I did not have to stay. It was my chance to carry out Thomas's plan. I dared not delay any longer. Sluggish with dread, I crossed the quadrangle that afternoon to inform Thomas that the time was ripe.

"Ah, at last." His eyes glittered. "Do you know where Bacon's quarters are?" I nodded. "A first-floor apartment—that'll make things simple," he continued. "One of the windows will have the shutters unlocked." He smiled, and his skin grew pinker.

"But—how can we be certain of that, Master Thomas?"

He cleared his throat. "The caretaker of that section happens to be in the employ of the Holy Office. I'll see that he gets a message."

My spirits were sinking lower with each second that passed. "How will I know which window?"

"Can't say—you'll have to use trial and error. Report back to me tomorrow. Don't look so glum, Brother Jean. There's nothing to this. And we're going to be successful,

that's what counts!"

I came away from Master Thomas's rooms with a churning stomach and an aching head. In a matter of hours, I was going to become a common sneak thief.

After Giles fell asleep that night, I put on my robe and moved as silently as I could out of the dormitory. A full moon threw the whole quadrangle into sharp focus. A bad sign—I could easily be seen. But there seemed to be few people about, most of them students scurrying back from a night on the town, one group giggling and chattering. I stayed in the shadows as much as possible until I reached the hall where Master Bacon resided, then stood studying the building.

A bell rang out, tolling the hour, and I jumped. Then I walked back and forth beneath Master Bacon's apartment, looking the place over. There were four windows opening onto the quadrangle, all dark. I tried first one window, then a second. No use—the shutters were locked. Was the night that warm, or was it my task that was making me damp with perspiration? A bird sang out, and my heart did a flip-flop.

I tried the shutters of the third window. They pulled back easily; they were not fastened. I breathed easier. The power of the Inquisition was far-reaching indeed. It was a low window, and I was able to hoist myself up through it in a moment. But I couldn't repress a shiver—what if someone was there?

Since I had no light, I had to depend on the moon-

light streaming through the open window. I seemed to be standing in a kind of study. On my left were a desk and a chair. On my right, a reading table centered in a wall of books. The moonlight did not quite reach the farthest wall of the room. I closed my eyes for a minute to get them used to the darkness. Then I moved slowly and quietly toward the back of the room. In one corner, I saw a shadowy something. My heart began to bang.

Something? No, not just something—a roundish object. A kind of statue. As I came even closer, I could see it was a bust. Was this the infamous bronze head that could speak? Sweat poured off of me, and my clothes stuck to my skin. What if it began to talk in a loud voice and attract attention? What would I do then? I took a deep breath, made the sign of the cross, and moved closer.

At that moment, a slight shuffling sound made me stop. A circle of light filled the room. Heart hammering now, I turned to flee. But between me and the window was a figure holding a lighted candle.

Master Roger Bacon stood there, looking at me. Fear froze me in place.

He came forward slowly, lifted the candle higher, and shifted his gaze from my face to the open window. "Jean? You? What are you doing here?"

My usually quick tongue could find no ready answer.

"Were you looking for me? Is something wrong?"

Still tongue-tied, I shook my head no. How could I ever explain? I was betraying a man I liked and trusted.

Master Bacon took me by the arm and led me over to one of the chairs. "Sit down." His voice was calm. He walked around the room, lighting a half dozen other candles that were already in place. The candlelight spread out a golden arc.

He placed another chair next to mine and sat. "Tell me, Jean, why are you here?" The question reminded me of the Grand Inquisitor, but Master Bacon's voice was not harsh.

I sat wrestling with my soul. I could make up some kind of story about needing his advice to help me out of some difficulty with the office of the *Decanus*—the dean of the university. Not finding him in, and being quite upset, I had found the open window and crawled in to wait for him. The knot of misery in my stomach reminded me that if I failed in my mission, I would soon have to face Master Thomas of York.

Yet as the false words rose to my lips, I could not speak them. By now I knew in my heart that Bacon was not a magician who played games with the Devil. Day in and day out, he worked tirelessly. I could see that Master Peckham was right. Master Bacon was a dedicated scholar, skilled in mathematics and the sciences. Moreover, with the same trust shown by Pierre de Maricourt, he had given me a place in his laboratory without questioning my motives. Men who trusted others were men of honor, I believed. I could not lie to him, even for the Church.

Master Bacon listened quietly as I told him everything,

from that first morning when I stood before the Grand Inquisitor to my last meeting with Thomas of York. After I finished, he shook his head in apparent wonderment. "I have been told that many people actually believe that the Devil works alongside me in my laboratory. Amazing that even among the most educated such superstitions persist! But I never thought they'd go so far as to use an innocent boy..."

I sat there, head hanging in misery and shame.

"Still," he went on, "we must consider the danger not only to you, but also to your loved ones. You will have to continue to report to that villain. Until we can think of some way to get you out from under the fist of the Holy Office."

"How can you do that? They'll never set me free until—" I did not know how to continue.

"Until they tie me to the stake, is that it?" His lips twisted in a derisive smile. He sat in silent thought for a moment. "Well, if it's the bronze head they're after, we'll have to come up with something that keeps them at bay for a while."

I had a flash of inspiration. "I could tell Master Thomas that Pierre de Maricourt borrowed the head from you and left Oxford with it."

"That's a good idea—he was my guest for a few days and then left for parts unknown. But no, it might put poor Petrus in a difficult position. They'd begin policing all the roads in England, and if they found him—"

"You're right. We can't put Pierre in jeopardy. You see," I added slowly, "from the moment I found out he was an alchemist, I was afraid of him. And when he showed me the lodestone, I was almost convinced he was an emissary of Satan. That's what comes from believing people's prattle. Pretty stupid of me, all right! I wish I could tell him—"

"Cheer up, you'll surely have a chance before you leave Oxford. Petrus is always turning up with some new discovery or other. Now to get back to our friend Master Thomas—what if you tell him that the head was not to be found in my living quarters here? But you have heard a rumor that I keep secret quarters in Oxford. Perhaps it's there. You'll try to follow me or Johannus whenever we go into town to find out where it is. Meanwhile, we'll put off going into town for some weeks. How does that sound?"

"Capital!" I felt better already. It was impossible to remain downhearted in the presence of this man.

Bacon laughed. "Good. That's settled. By the way, when I came in, you were looking at that bust by the wall, weren't you?"

My face grew hot. "I was afraid it might be—"

"—the chatty bronze head, of course. Well, come take a closer look at it."

I rose and walked over to the bust, which looked more like plaster than bronze. It was a solemn, bearded face, with wisdom written all over it. The sightless eyes seemed

to bore into mine. I dropped my gaze to the letters etched at the base.

They spelled the name of the great Greek philosopher whose works were studied by Oxford students in almost all our university courses: ARISTOTLE.

CHAPTER NINE

Master Thomas of York was not happy.

"What? You found no sign of the accursed bronze head in Bacon's quarters? Damnation! You looked in every room?"

"Yes, Master Thomas, every room."

"And what about what goes on in the laboratory? Any new evidence? Incantations? Pentagrams?"

I shook my head. "Just ordinary alchemical preparations. Believe me, I know the whole routine there. But I've been unable to detect any signs of black magic whatsoever."

"Damnation!" he repeated. "We've got to find a way."

"I have an idea, if you don't mind my suggesting it."

"Oh? What might that be?"

"I've heard rumors that Master Bacon has a secret place somewhere in Oxford—a place where he stores things. I could follow him when he goes into town. Perhaps the bronze head—"

"Capital!" he interrupted, rubbing his hands together. "But don't try to enter the place by yourself. When you discover it, bring me the address, and I'll arrange for a search."

His mood was greatly improved. Nevertheless, he didn't hesitate to remind me of my predicament. "We'd better find that head soon, Brother Jean. Remember that your scholarship hangs on the success of our mission. And perhaps more than that."

I cleared my throat. "Master Thomas, perhaps—uh—perhaps Master Bacon isn't guilty."

"What? What kind of talk is this!" Thomas roared. "Oh, these heretics are clever. They know how to cast spells over the innocent! I don't want to hear such nonsense again!"

I hung my head as I left. I wasn't brave enough to battle Master Thomas. To argue with him and the Holy Office was not only hopeless, but also dangerous. Probably fatal.

When I mentioned to Master Bacon the possibility that my scholarship might be canceled, he shrugged my anxiety

away. "That's no problem. I can arrange for your costs to be covered quite easily. You see, Oxford has the Frideswide Chest."

"The Fride—?"

He smiled. "No one's told you about that, eh? Well, Oxford was founded on the site of an old nunnery called Saint Frideswide's. And in memory of that place, the Church arranged for a special chest to be always filled with money for the support of poor but deserving students. That's the Frideswide Chest. I'm sure that we can arrange to help you!"

"Thank you, Master Bacon, that's a great relief. Though I don't know why you should do all that for me. I've done nothing but try to do you harm."

Master Bacon dismissed my protest with a wave of his hand. "Let's not worry about what may never happen. Now blow the furnace up, so that I can cook what's in this pelican for a little while longer."

I began spending more time in the laboratory, and my absence became a sore point with Giles. "First Ian goes, and now I'm losing you to that magician. I'm worried about you, Jean. People keep talking about Bacon being in league with Satan. And there are reports of strange noises and weird lights over where you work. I know it's none of my business, but—"

"Come on, Giles, you don't really believe that nonsense, do you? I've been working in that laboratory for some

time now. Let me tell you, Master Bacon is no more a magician than you or I! He's a true man of science, trying to find the causes of what happens in nature. As for those weird noises and lights, I'll bet that happens in any alchemist's laboratory."

Giles gave a sigh. "It's a relief to hear you say that, Jean. I was honestly afraid that you'd been won over by the Devil, and that one day you'd disappear in a puff of smoke!"

I gave him a playful punch in the arm. "Serve you right if I did. And maybe I'd take you with me!"

Giles laughed, but then his face became serious again. "You should know that there is one master at Oxford who whispers it about that Bacon is the Antichrist himself come to earth."

I did not realize that Thomas of York had gone to such extremes as to suggest that Bacon was the Antichrist. According to the Holy Book, the Antichrist was a dreadful being who would come to power some time before the day of the Last Judgment—the day the world would end. And his mission would be to sway the final battle between the forces of good and evil, so that evil would win out. "You mean Thomas of York, Giles?"

"How did you know?"

"I hear the same rumors. Do you know what Bacon says about Master York? 'He's a man so ignorant of science, he thinks experimenting to learn about nature is practicing black magic!'" I was not about to tell Giles of

my secret connection with Thomas of York. It was enough that Bacon and Johannus knew.

When I came to the laboratory the following evening, Johannus handed me a piece of parchment. On it were printed eight words: SALIS PETRAE LURU VOPO VIR CAN UTRIET SULPHURIS. I knew what the first two words meant; they were the Latin for saltpeter, or niter. And the last word was sulfur. But the five words in between made no sense at all. "What does it mean, Johannus?"

He grinned. "I see you haven't learned about challenges yet. When someone in the university world makes a discovery of some sort, he doesn't announce it directly. Instead, he writes a sentence describing the discovery and rearranges the letters into an anagram. The anagram is sent to his associates as a challenge—to figure out what has been discovered."

"What a strange game!"

"It's fun, wait till you see. Come, let's go over to where the master is working—he'll translate it for you."

Master Bacon was seated at his bench, weighing out some powders.

"Here's our helper," Johannus grinned. "And he's already failed the course in anagrams."

Master Bacon carefully emptied the white powder he was weighing into a mortar before speaking. "Well, we'll have to give him more practice at the game. Look here, Jean." He picked up a pen and wrote on the parchment

Johannus had placed on the table. "Suppose we rearrange the letters like this:

L U R U V O P O V I R C A N U T R I E T
R. V I P A R T. V N O V C O R U L I E T

then the whole message becomes:

SALIS PETRAE R. VI PART. V NOV. CORULI ET SULPHURIS—"

As Master Bacon spoke, the letters had been twisting themselves in my mind. Suddenly it was all clear. "I've got it! The R stands for the word that begins all alchemical formulas—*Recipe*. So that says 'Take six parts of saltpeter, and five parts each of young willow'—that's charcoal, isn't it?—'and sulfur.' Right?"

"Well done, Jean!" Master Bacon smiled and patted me on the back.

"But where did you find this formula? What happens when you combine these earths?" And to think that not long ago I'd believed anagrams were part of witchcraft!

"Pierre carried it all the way from the land of the Saracens. When these things are mixed and placed in a—well, Johannus, we might as well show him." Master Bacon showed me the mortar into which he'd poured the white stuff he'd been weighing. From two other jars, he measured out the black charcoal and yellow sulfur and

poured them into the mortar. Then, with the pestle, he stirred the mixture slowly. "You must mix these very carefully, until the mixture is of one color. Mind, no heavy rubbing."

He moved the pestle round and round. Slowly, the separate colors became a uniform gray. Using a sharp knife, Master Bacon cut a square out of a blank piece of parchment and placed a small amount of the mixture onto the square. He deftly rolled the parchment into a tube and twisted the ends to keep the powder from spilling.

"Johannus, a flame, please."

Johannus picked a long splinter of wood from a pile, took it over to the furnace, and brought it back flaming to the master. Master Bacon took it and held the flame to one end of the tube. The parchment sizzled and sputtered for a moment. Then the tube exploded with a brilliant flash and a deafening bang that made my ears ring. A foul-smelling smoke filled the laboratory.

Impulsively I crossed myself. "Holy Mother of God!"

A sudden pounding on the door sent Johannus on the run to open it. A half dozen frightened faces peered in. "What happened? We heard a thunderclap!"

Johannus raised his hand. "Nothing to worry about, fellows, nothing at all. Just a little experiment that got a bit noisy. No damage. . . no one hurt. Thank you for your concern. Good-bye."

The faces departed amidst murmurs of, "...that magi-

cian at it again...fourth time this week...probably calling up Lucifer himself..."

Master Bacon looked at me with a boyish grin splitting his face. "Well, the formula seems to work. I think it's time to prepare a special lecture for my colleagues. Let me see..." He scratched at one ear. "Johannus, find out when the Great Hall is free next week." He turned to me. "Jean, make it a point to see Thomas of York and inform him that I'll be giving a lecture on the subject of magic."

"Magic? You mean black magic?" The very words worried me.

CHAPTER TEN

Johannus stifled a giggle as Roger Bacon shook his head. "No, magic of quite a different kind. And we'll cap the lecture with a demonstration of the power of our new formula."

On the appointed afternoon, the Great Hall of the university overflowed with students and faculty. The news that Master Bacon was to give one of his famous lectures had traveled about the campus as though yoked to the winged sandals of Mercury. The senior students were busy gossiping about how a Roger Bacon lecture was always good for a surprise.

Faculty members sat in the front rows of benches reserved for them. Behind them, students filled not only the benches, but also the stairs and doorways. A loud buzz of excited voices echoed throughout the hall. But as Master Bacon entered, followed by Johannus and me, the buzz trailed off and stopped. Every eye was riveted upon us.

Johannus carried a candle and a small tray on which sat a rolled tube of parchment about six inches long, with twisted ends. He placed the tray on the small table in the center of the floor and took the candle back with him. Master Bacon had arranged for two chairs so that we could sit behind him. I caught the eye of Thomas of York in the front row. He nodded slightly as if to let me know I was carrying out my task well. I caught a glimpse of Giles in the front row—I had persuaded him to attend.

"Fellow masters and students," Master Bacon began in his clear voice, "you are here because this lecture was announced as one dealing with magic. I hope you will not be disappointed to learn that the lecture will not be about the kind of magic you are probably picturing—black magic. No, gentlemen, this lecture will be a *denial* of black magic. We are all scholars. Isn't it time we got rid of all silly superstitions? Should we really believe that Satan and his demons, in exchange for our souls, will teach us how to manipulate nature? No, fellow scholars, we cannot force nature to do things it cannot do!"

"Blasphemy!" called out Thomas of York. "What about

the miracles in the Bible?"

"A point well taken, Master Thomas. But I am not talking about the power of God. In His wisdom He created the heavens and earth and humanity. I'm sure we all agree that God's power is beyond our knowledge."

"But Satan has the power to subvert nature! And you know all about that kind of power!" cried a voice from the faculty benches.

I was taken aback. How would Bacon handle this accusation that he was a bedfellow of the Devil?

Master Bacon only raised his eyebrows and smiled. "I am not one of those who claim they can control nature through some spell that raises up Satan. No, I begin with the following proposition: when God made humans, he also gave them brains. Now, why did God do that? Let me tell you why. The human brain was to be used for the acquisition of knowledge!"

A mutter ran through the audience, and Bacon paused until it had passed.

"And God also gave us a curiosity about nature so that our brains could be exercised by thinking. Now some of you may believe that the only means of understanding nature is through what God reveals to us. But I put it to you that there is a better way to understand nature. *By gathering facts about nature through experimentation*. Experiments that let us find out how nature behaves can lead us to finding out how to control nature. And such knowledge, my fellow scholars, is the kind of power

humans must acquire!"

Bacon paused. The voice of Thomas of York broke through the silence again. "This is all nonsense! There is nothing about this in all of Aristotle's writings!"

"Aristotle!" Bacon spat the name back at his heckler. "Are we scholars only sponges that sop up Aristotle's words as though he were a god?"

A gasp went up from the audience. How could this man say such a thing about Aristotle, the great authority of old, whose words were almost as sacred to scholars as those of the Holy Book itself?

A few daring students in the rear benches applauded and called "*Bene dictus*—well said!" But most of the faculty turned to glare at them, muttering the word that judges of the Inquisition used to condemn heretics to the flames, *"Damnatus! Damnatus!"*

Bacon continued as if he had not heard. "If we use what I call *natural* magic, we can control nature. How can we learn by this kind of magic? By using our senses to observe and our brains to reason. There is no end to the possibilities of using such magic to unlock the secrets of nature, and thus make things undreamed of come to pass!"

Thomas of York stretched his arms and uttered a loud and prolonged yawn. "Are we to be lulled to sleep by these fantasies?"

"No fantasies, my friend. I will now reveal to you a behavior of nature that I am certain you have never seen before. And in keeping with academic custom, I give you

an anagram of this behavior and challenge you to decipher it." Bacon strode over and handed Thomas a piece of parchment.

Thomas scanned what was written. "Luru vopo vir—?" He flung the parchment to the floor. "I have no time for childish conundrums!"

"Well, Master Thomas, since you don't seem to enjoy anagrams, I'll present what that means directly." Bacon moved the tray holding the fat tube to the center of the table. "Johannus, the candle, please."

Johannus rose and gave the candle to Bacon. All eyes in the hall were riveted on the alchemist as he held the flame to one twisted end of the parchment. When the parchment caught and began to sputter, he walked casually away toward a corner of the room, beckoning us to follow.

The sputtering stopped. Not a sound could be heard in the Great Hall. I held my breath.

In the silence, Thomas began to speak. "What kind of—"

He got no further. The Great Hall blazed with a tremendous flash of lightning. A crash of thunder echoed around the walls. A thick smoke poured out, filling our nostrils with that sulfurous stench.

Screaming and shoving, students and faculty alike leaped from their seats and dashed for the exits. Some sat stunned for a moment, holding their hands to their ears, but they soon joined the mob fighting to get out.

Thomas of York, dignity thrown to the winds, was hurling aside those in his path. Some students with knives out were pricking the backs of those in front to hurry them on.

Above the hubbub could be heard cries of, "The Devil! I saw him in the smoke! No, it was the Antichrist!"

Roger Bacon watched it all, calm as ever, with a smile on his face. Johannus, too, was chuckling to himself. But all I could think of was that Bacon now had more enemies than ever before.

And that Thomas of York finally had the evidence he needed for the Grand Inquisitor.

CHAPTER ELEVEN

That night, both Giles and I found it hard to fall asleep. We tossed on our pallets, mulling over Bacon's extraordinary lecture.

"I'm ashamed, Jean. What on earth made me panic like the rest of those scared idiots!"

"Look, anybody would be scared the first time. I'd have turned tail and run, too, if I hadn't known what was coming. You should've seen me when it happened in the laboratory!"

"Just what was in that tube?"

"A formula that came all the way from the Saracens—

saltpeter, charcoal, and sulfur. Amazing, isn't it!"

"But what good is it? A mixture that makes explosions?" Giles changed his tack. "Just the same, you seem to be enjoying your work over there. But handling stuff that explodes—isn't that dangerous?"

"Not so far—and it's exciting. I'm learning things about nature that I never knew before. Maybe the formula could be useful, who knows?"

Giles yawned. "Better get some sleep—they'll be waking us for morning Mass in about a minute."

But I was still awake after Giles dropped off. A thousand questions were buzzing through my brain. What could Bacon do with that Saracen formula, apart from creating useless thunder and lightning? And why had he chosen to offend Thomas of York so openly? Didn't Bacon fear the power of the Holy Office as I did—as everyone did? Such a brilliant man! But he seemed to walk in a pure world of his own. Perhaps he underestimated how fearful Thomas of York and his cronies were of any challenge to long-established ideas.

When Giles and I returned to St. Edmund's at lunchtime, there was a letter awaiting him. He tore it open anxiously. "From my father—why is he writing again so soon?" As he read the first lines, his face fell.

"What's wrong, Giles?"

"He's gone off to join the army of Simon de Montfort. To fight the king!"

"Why are they against the king?"

"Because he broke his promises to the barons to give up his power to them. And the free Londoners—my father's one of them—hate the king, too. So they've joined up with de Montfort to go down to the town of Lewes in the south of England."

"And will you join them there?"

"Yes." Giles folded the letter. "But first to London, to see how Mother is. Then off to Lewes to stand by my father's side." He began stuffing clothes into his pack.

"But Giles, what about your courses here at the university?"

"My father's life is more important! And that letter was sent over a week ago." He put aside his pack. "Will you give me your blessing, Jean?"

"Blessing?" I stared at him. Could I really stay here, studying quietly, while my best friend was going into battle? "Wait!" I bent and retrieved my pack. "I'll do better than that. I'll go with you."

"You? What for? You're a Frenchman—this quarrel has no meaning for you."

"True. But you're my best friend. And you need a companion on the road for safety."

Giles grasped my hand. "Well, then, what are we waiting for? Let's go!"

In the corridor, I stopped. "Shouldn't we tell someone that we'll be away? We'll be missing a number of lectures."

"Who? Master Peckham will never agree—"

"I've got it! Let's tell Master Bacon. He'll find a way to cover for us."

I almost had to drag Giles into the laboratory. He was still fearful of the place and refused to move more than a foot inside the door. His eyes kept roaming anxiously over the blazing furnace and the shelves overflowing with equipment and materials.

Both Bacon and Johannus tried to show us the foolhardiness of what we were about to do. But I stood my ground. "Giles is my friend—I can't let him go alone."

Finally Bacon said, "Very well, Jean, go with my blessing. We'll find some way to cover for you both. But be careful. War is terrible."

It took Giles and me only a few minutes to cross the quadrangle, dash through the gates to the nearest livery stable, and hire a pair of horses. Late in the afternoon of the second day on the road, we entered through the gate into London. As Giles led the way to his house, I remembered the time I had first seen London Bridge and the heads of criminals mounted on pikes.

The Rowley house sat in one of the more opulent sections of the city, across from a park. As we clattered through the gate, a groom came out to see to our horses. But as soon as a pretty young girl opened the door, I knew something was wrong. Her face was sorrowful, her eyes red. "Oh, Giles, thank God you're home!" She hurled herself into his arms.

"What is it, Sally? What's happened? Where's Mother?"

"Giles?" A slender woman with a coronet of fair hair came into the hall from an adjoining room. She was dressed in black. Sally stood weeping.

Giles clasped her in his arms. "Mother! What's happened?"

"Oh, Giles, I was just sitting down to write to you." She pulled away but held on to Giles's hands. "It's your father—we've had word—"

"He's been hurt!"

Mrs. Rowley shook her head. "Oh, Giles, he's dead! We've lost him!" Her lips quivered. I could see she was making a tremendous effort not to cry. Sally stopped weeping and dabbed at her eyes with a kerchief.

Giles had a disbelieving look on his face. "Dead? But that's impossible!" He pulled the letter from his pocket. "He wrote to me—"

"We heard yesterday afternoon. He died bravely, they said, along with many of the other Londoners." Her gaze fell on me, and she straightened her shoulders. "And this young man?"

Giles introduced me to his mother and sister. "Jean refused to let me travel alone."

"That was kind of you, Jean," said his mother. "And you are more than welcome to stay with us."

"Oh, no," I said, "this is no time for you to be burdened with guests. I'll start back for Oxford."

"Jean," said Giles, putting his arm out as if to bar my way, "let's hear no such nonsense. Of course you'll

stay." He was struggling to control himself; his eyes were wet. "Besides, we'll need your help."

Two days later, a cart carrying the body of Giles's father arrived. I stayed at the Rowley house long enough to attend the funeral service, then I bade them good-bye. Mrs. Rowley thanked me again for accompanying her son. She and Sally assured me I would always be welcome in their home.

In the courtyard, astride my horse, I said good-bye to Giles. "What will you do about the university? When will you come back to Oxford?"

"Back? Never." Giles shook his head. "I must stay and see to my father's business affairs. I'll have to take care of my mother and Sally." He looked up at me. "You're the only one of our triad who'll be getting an education. Just don't forget your illiterate friends."

I leaned over and took Giles's hand. "It won't be the same without you."

He smiled. "Remember, if you need my help for anything at all, I'll come."

I waved to Sally and turned my horse toward the gate. It was high time for me to get back to Oxford, even though my two best friends would no longer be there with me. It struck me that all three of us were fatherless now.

Three afternoons later, I left the horse at the livery stable in Oxford and headed for the university gates. I was astonished to find Johannus sitting on the steps outside St. Edmund's.

He leaped to his feet. "Jean! Thank God you're here!"

"What is it, Johannus? What's wrong?"

"I've come every day hoping to find you back. Jean, a terrible thing has happened. Master Bacon has been arrested and taken away!"

CHAPTER TWELVE

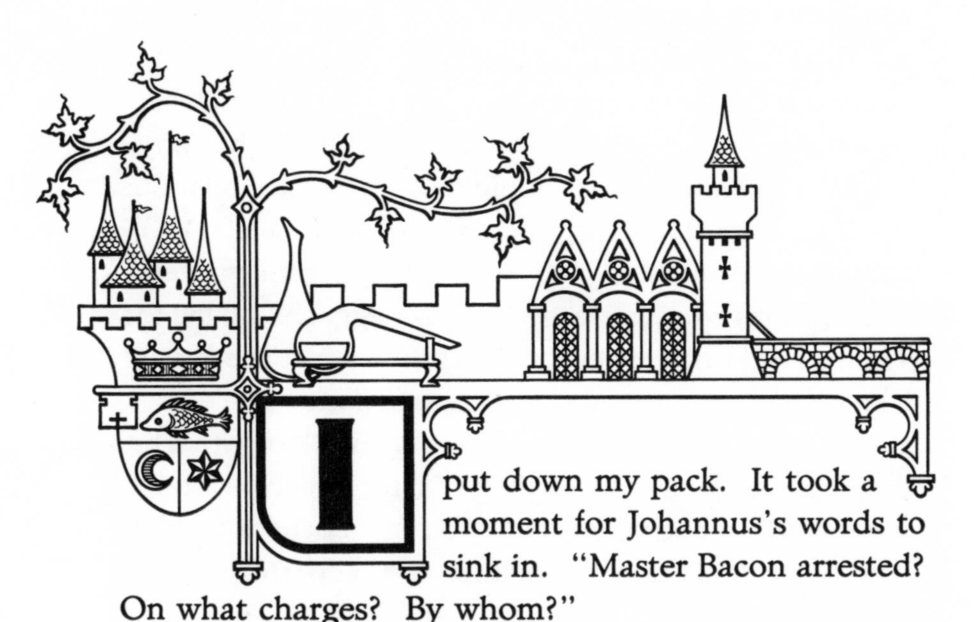

I put down my pack. It took a moment for Johannus's words to sink in. "Master Bacon arrested? On what charges? By whom?"

"I don't even know! One day, a Franciscan and a Dominican showed up at the laboratory with two guards from the Oxford Holy Office. They read off some gibberish about proof of heresy from a document they waved around. And then they just grabbed him and marched him off! When I tried to stop them, one of the guards stuck the point of his halberd under my nose and ordered me to keep out of it."

"When did all this happen?"

"It's almost a week now."

"Have you gone to the dean to find out about it?"

"I ran there right away! But they kept me waiting for hours. Finally, the dean came out and said the matter was out of his hands—official Church business." He gave me an anguished look. "Jean, we can't let them keep him in some godforsaken place! He's not a young man, what'll become of him! We've got to do something right away."

I put my hand on his shoulder. "Patience, Johannus. We'll have to think this out. There must be a way."

"It's the fault of all those stupid, ignorant masters!" Johannus raged. He reached for his dagger. "I'll kill that Thomas of York! He egged them on against the Master, I know it!" He waved the dagger around.

This was a Johannus I had never seen. "Stop it! Then you'll be in worse trouble than Master Bacon! Listen to me. Wouldn't it be better if you stayed here to make sure those fools don't vandalize the laboratory? What do you think?"

"Oh, Pierre thought of that right away. He's there now."

"Pierre is back in Oxford? When did he come?"

"The day after they took the master. Thank God he's here!"

The weariness from a long day in the saddle suddenly overwhelmed me. "Johannus, I must rest. Tomorrow I'll come to the laboratory as soon as I can. Stop worrying.

We'll figure something out."

He nodded and turned to go. "I'll tell Pierre you're back. See you tomorrow. We've got to work fast." It was a different Johannus without his usual cheerful grin.

When I stopped off to let the master of St. Edmund's know of my return, he handed me a sealed note. It turned out to be from Thomas of York, ordering me to report to him at once. I stuck the note in my pack, went to my room in the dormitory, and soon groaned with the relief of being able to stretch out on my own bed. Master Thomas of York could wait. Of course, I'd have to face his anger. But I was too tired to worry about it.

Next morning, I awoke too late for Mass. As for Master Peckham's lecture, I decided it would be more prudent to visit him later in the day and ask about what I had missed. Nor was I ready to face Master Thomas. Instead, I headed for Bacon's laboratory.

Pierre de Maricourt was working there by himself, and his greeting was exuberant. "Welcome, Jean! It's wonderful to see you again."

Remembering how I had fled like a thief in the night from the inn, I found it hard to respond. "It's a little late, but I want to apologize—"

He laughed. "Apology accepted. I knew you were a young man in a hurry."

"Thank you for being so understanding. But what are we going to do about Master Bacon?"

"What indeed. The Holy Office is not easily thwarted."

He rubbed his chin. "To get him out of their hands seems impossible."

"I know how the Holy Office works." The interview with Thomas of York awaited me. "As for what's impossible, God has been known to make the impossible possible."

He clapped me on the shoulder. "A good thought to keep in mind, Jean. Well, Johannus told me about your problem with the Holy Office. But there must be a way to deal with that, too."

"Do you know where they've taken him?"

"Yes. To a dungeon on the coast of France. Near Dunquerque."

"We can't let him rot in a place like that!" I was truly alarmed at this news. "Look, I've got to go see Master Thomas of York first. As soon as I'm finished, I'll be back here. Who knows, maybe I can pry something out of him that'll be useful."

Pierre's eyebrows rose. "Good luck! Johannus will be here by then, so we'll have three heads to work things out."

Master Thomas's greeting was far from friendly. "Where have you been? You left Oxford without letting me know!"

"Forgive me, Master Thomas. My roommate, Giles Rowley, had a family emergency. I went along to help him. Of course I should have notified you, but there was no time."

"Hmph. Well, by now I presume you've heard what's

happened to Roger Bacon?"

"He was taken by the Holy Office—?"

"Yes." The word came out like a long hiss. "With the assistance of both the Franciscan and the Dominican orders." He leaned back in his chair and chuckled. "I knew that he was bound to give himself away, and he did! That last lecture, with that devilish thunder and lightning—"

"And that was enough to prove him a heretic?"

"More than enough! With half the faculty there to witness it—and swear they had seen the Foul Fiend in the smoke!" Thomas sat back, grinning.

Like Johannus, my first thought was to dash back for my dagger and put an end to this idiot's grin. But thoughts of my uncle and aunt drove the idea from my mind. "I hear they've taken Master Bacon out of England."

"Yes, to a French dungeon. Run by his own order, the Franciscans. What d'you think of that for a joke!" He laughed at his own remark. "He'll have plenty of time to repent his wickedness!"

"How like the Holy Order, they've thought of everything." I frowned. "But if he has the power to summon up demons, how can they hold him there? What kind of guards do they have?"

"Ah, he's in a cell high up on the sea side, atop a stone wall. It would be impossible to scale it. And the guards are recruited from the local forces, specially trained in the

art of dispersing demons. No, there'll be no more theatrical exhibitions by Master Bacon!" He rubbed his plump hands together with glee.

"He'll never escape, that's for sure." I prayed I was wrong.

"No thanks to you." Thomas eyed me. "For my part, you didn't do your job. You never came up with a shred of evidence against Bacon. But the matter's all settled now—we've got the heretic. So we need have no more meetings. You're dismissed."

Relief flooded through me. "Thank you, Master Thomas." I stood up, free at last.

"Wait, one thing more. Your scholarship was originally meant for the University of Paris, I understand. Now that this affair is finished, you can write to your abbot in Toulouse and ask to have the scholarship transferred from Oxford. Just think—you'll be attending a university run by our own order! Maybe that'll knock some sense into your head!"

"The University of Paris—a chance to sit at the feet of Thomas Aquinas." It was what I had always dreamed of. I thanked Master Thomas again and left.

As I crossed the quadrangle on my way to the laboratory, I found myself being eyed by many as an object of curiosity. One or two of the masters showed what they thought of Bacon's apprentice by deliberately stepping out of my path and crossing themselves as I passed. I paid them little attention.

Johannus had returned to the laboratory, and I relayed to him and Pierre the information I had gotten from Thomas of York. When I told them of my deliverance from the yoke of the Inquisition, they beamed and clapped me on the back.

"Good news, Jean!" cried Johannus.

"Now we have to find a way to do the same for Roger," said Pierre. "Let's sit and put on our thinking caps." We followed his advice.

"A high sea wall right on the water," murmured Johannus. "That means we can't do it from outside the prison."

"Right," said Pierre, "we have to find a way to get in."

"And having done that," I added, "we have to get him—and ourselves—out!" A germ of an idea began to form in my mind. "Pierre, you're a man of the world. Do you by chance know of a good counterfeiter around here? One who could forge a creditable Church document?"

Pierre scratched his chin. "A forger? Let me think... yes, there is such a one right here in Oxford. Why do you ask?"

"Could you persuade him to contrive an official order from the Holy Office in Rome? Stating that Roger Bacon is to be handed over to the bearer for questioning?"

Johannus sat up. "You mean we could pretend to be—"

I finished the sentence. "Agents of the Holy Office? Why not? I'm well acquainted with the Grand Inquisitor of Toulouse. I recall his manner only too well. What do

you say, Pierre?"

"I say it's a real possibility. Good work, Jean. But is there more to your plan?"

"Yes. We'll need strength on our side, in case something unexpected occurs. I'll send word to my good friend Ian MacIver, in Scotland. He's a brave giant of a man. If it should come to swordplay, he's the one we want on our side."

Johannus drummed his fingers impatiently on the table. "But we have to get across the Channel to Dunquerque. That'll cost money."

"I know." I looked at Pierre.

He pursed his lips. "Fellows, at the moment I'm a bit strapped for cash. But I know someone who might lend—"

I held up my hand. "Wait, I have a better idea. My roommate, Giles Rowley, is in London now tending to his father's business, after his father was killed at the battle of Lewes. Giles has said that if I ever needed his help, I had only to ask. He'll find a way to get us a ship, I'm sure."

"Good," said Pierre, "now there are four of us."

"Five!" Johannus put in sharply.

"Johannus, listen." I reached across the table to touch his hand. "Someone must stay here to guard Master Bacon's possessions. While we're gone, your job will be to think of how we can hide him afterward, while we're trying to get his sentence revoked."

"But I want to be there when—" Johannus began.

"Of course you do," I interrupted. "But you can really do Master Bacon more good by watching this place." Johannus's face fell, but he nodded his agreement. I turned to Pierre. "One more thing. You can't be an agent of the Holy Office in Rome dressed as a Franciscan. Can you get hold of a Dominican robe somewhere?"

"Here in Oxford?" Pierre shook his head. "There aren't many Dominicans here."

"Thomas of York's a Dominican! D'you think he might have an extra robe in his wardrobe at New College?" I winked at Pierre.

He winked back. "It's a distinct possibility."

"Good!" I leaned back in my chair and regarded my fellow plotters. "Once we have the forged document and the Dominican robe—and as soon as Ian gets here—we'll be on our way. Meanwhile, I'll write to Giles to prepare him for what's ahead. Now, supposing all goes well—we get inside the dungeon and they take us to Master Bacon's cell—here's my idea for the rest of it."

Pierre and Johannus leaned forward as I bent my head and described my plan.

"By God," exclaimed Pierre when I had finished, "that's a stroke of genius! To use Bacon's exploding powder to get him out!"

"It's perfect!" Johannus seemed excited. "And that way I can really help! I know how to prepare it!"

Pierre slapped me on the back. "You've come a long

way, lad. Remember when you asked me about the vow of obedience? Whether there might be a time when blind obedience could be wrong? Well, I see that your little encounter with the Holy Office has made you see the light!"

We all looked at each other. And in silence, three hands came together at the center of the table in a gesture of friendship and determination.

CHAPTER THIRTEEN

Time passed slowly. Finally one day, Ian MacIver's huge bulk appeared in the doorway of the laboratory. "Is it safe fer a body t'enter these fiendish premises?" He was staring at the jars and crucibles.

I shouted with joy. "Ian, you're here! Nothing to fear, you idiot—come on in. Are we glad to see you!" I introduced him to Johannus and Pierre, who both beamed at the idea of having him on our side.

Ian's air of apprehension vanished. "Your letter only said ye had grievous need of me. What's going on?"

I took Ian aside and told him everything, from my

ensnarement by the Holy Office to Bacon's arrest. "Master Bacon is a man of science, not the evil magician that people whisper he is. And it's up to me to make amends for having spied on him. We've got to get him out of that dungeon!"

"Indeed, and how d'ye intend to do that, laddie?"

I laid out the plan for him. "We couldn't do it without you, Ian. We've got to have a man-at-arms for protection. My idea is to tell them that you're one of the special guards of the Holy Order."

Ian grinned. "Is it action, then, that ye're promising me? Sure I'll come along with ye. And Giles will be coming too, ye say?"

Just having Ian there raised my spirits. "Yes, it's the three of us together again! Plus Pierre—he'll be a great help. And Johannus will hold the fort here."

By the end of the following week, the forged document was ready—a handsome job that anyone would have sworn was printed in the Vatican, with all the correct seals duplicated exactly. A letter finally arrived from Giles, who agreed to take part in rescuing Bacon. He was combing the wharves of the Thames, he wrote, for a reliable boatman. And we were not to worry about the cost, he said.

One important detail still remained—to borrow one of Thomas of York's robes. Pierre assured us that he could manage this with no trouble. By this time, he had made a study of Thomas's habits. Sure enough, the night before we were ready to depart for London, Pierre turned up with

the robe.

"How on earth did you manage to get into his locked quarters?" I asked.

Pierre smiled. "Remember the goliards, the wandering scholars? One of them is an accomplished thief who has a way with locked doors."

I shook my head in astonishment over what Pierre had achieved. "Thank heavens no one got caught!" A fine irony, too, to have Master Thomas's robe help save Roger Bacon! The act itself was illegal enough, to be sure. But why should such a trifling matter bother me, when I was already committed to an entire illegal plot to save Bacon? Here I was, going against my order as well as the Holy Office. Perhaps what had started me on this path was remembering how they had accused me of heresy when I was completely innocent. Like me, Bacon was a victim of lies.

The chilly fingers of autumn had brushed the fields of Oxford with frost on the morning we set out. White vapor blew from our horses' nostrils and from our mouths. Once outside the city, we turned to the southeast and headed for London.

At the Rowleys' home, we were heartily welcomed by Giles and his mother, who still wore mourning clothes. When I introduced her to Ian and Pierre, she bade them welcome and, since it was already late, called to one of the maids to make our bedchambers ready.

"But Madame Rowley—" Pierre had already won her

over by kissing her hand in the French manner. "We thank you, but we had planned to stop at an inn." I knew he meant the inn of the Grillers, where he and I had stayed together.

"I won't hear of any such thing!" She frowned at the very notion. "You're Giles's friends, and you're staying with us. Besides, Giles's sister is away visiting cousins in Devon, so there's plenty of room."

We were tired enough to give in. Ian and Pierre shared one room, Giles and I another. "What about the boat?" I asked Giles. "All set?"

"Done! We can leave tomorrow if you wish. The boatman is a rogue, but a master sailor. He'll get us across safely."

"Good work, Giles. But what about the cost?"

Giles waved his hand. "Don't worry about it. My father's business is doing well, so that's no problem. Now, your letter was rather sketchy. What's the plan, once we get to France?"

He listened while I told him. But on one point he disagreed strongly. "No, I want to go inside the prison with you!"

"But Giles, we need someone to stay outside in case something goes wrong. We don't know what condition Master Bacon's in—we may have to carry him. If we're being chased, you can help Ian hold them off while we get Bacon to the boat."

He thought for a moment. "Maybe you're right. Ian

can handle any trouble inside, and I'll take care of it outside. Very well, let's get some sleep."

But I was too excited for sleep. Was the plan a sound one? Thoughts of what we had to do and what might go wrong zigzagged back and forth through my head. But I must have slept finally, because suddenly Giles's hand was shaking me. "Wake up, Jean! Mother has breakfast waiting."

Pierre and Ian were already downstairs, wolfing down porridge, bread, bacon, and eggs at a polished round table. We joined them and enjoyed Mrs. Rowley's hospitality, as she made sure that we ate heartily. When it was time to leave, she embraced each of us in turn. To me she whispered, "You'll take care of Giles, won't you?" Her arms about me were comforting, and her warm wishes seemed a talisman for luck.

The way her gaze lingered on her son, it was certainly brave of her to let him join our expedition so soon after losing her husband. I wondered if she would rest easy until Giles returned. I envied Giles that concern, heaven help me.

Servants had brought our horses out of the barn. A few minutes later, we were following Giles to the banks of the Thames. We left our horses at the nearest livery stable and walked to the small wharf where the boat was tied. It was a smaller boat than the one that had survived the storm to carry Pierre and me to England.

The boatman's name was Sam Seabury. He was an old

rascal whose first words to us were, "Ye can tell by my name where I'll be buried when I go!" Seeing my expression when I looked at his frail craft, he added, "The *London Belle*'s small, but she's trim. And she'll get ye where ye're goin'."

"How close to the dungeon can you get us?" I asked.

"Come aboard and I'll show ye." We followed him over the side and to the small forecastle. He went in and returned in a moment with a piece of parchment. "Drew a map, so's ye can tell." He pointed. "Now I know this piece of shore well, mind ye. Good place to bring in goods without payin' taxes to them French bloodsuckers. Here's yer dungeon, see. Wall comes right up to the water. And here, 'bout a hunnerd yards or so away, is a small cove. Good beach for goin' ashore. Hidden by a bunch o' them tall trees they grows there—"

"Poplars," said Pierre.

"Them's the ones. Well, that's where I picks ye up when ye're done with yer business. Remember, ye goes straight down the road from the dungeon 'bout a hunnerd yards or so. Take a right through the trees, and I'll be waitin'."

We all looked at each other. Pierre shrugged. "Sounds good to me," he said.

"Then we're off!" Sam gave a shout that brought a sailor who had been lurking nearby running to the boat. They hoisted the big square sail and pushed off from the wharf. After we had drifted about twenty feet into the

Thames, the west wind caught the sail and began to move us downstream. As we passed under London Bridge, I remembered the heads of the king's enemies on the pikes.

Even though it was still quite early, the Thames River was already bustling with boat traffic—from long barges to great merchant ships. Seabury kept calling out orders to the sailor who was handling the steering oar. "Hard aport! Steady as she goes! Damn yer eyes, get over t' starboard!" The last was to a merchant ship moving upstream that had wandered out of its channel toward us.

"We'll be out o' this mess soon's we get past Margate and into the Strait," he assured us. "Looks like the wind's right today—get us to Dunquerque easy as pie."

"Och," Ian whispered in my ear, "what's the Strait?"

"Strait of Dover. Hope we don't run into the Cinque Ports pirates."

"Pirates? Och, lad, how d'ye know about them?"

"Heard about them on the boat to England," I said. "A pretty bloody lot, they say."

Ian patted the sword hanging from his belt. "Don't give it a thought, lad. We'll be ready for 'em."

Did I envy him his weapon? But I was only to play assistant to an emissary of the Holy Office. Angrily I told myself that my part was just as important as Ian's.

Good fortune smiled on us as we sailed out of the mouth of the Thames and headed south into the Channel. The waters were fairly calm and the wind straight out of the northwest, carrying us right across the Strait to our

destination.

Seabury first took the *London Belle* into the cove he had drawn on his map. "This is it. I'll anchor the ship offshore and row in t' pick ye up in that." He jerked his thumb over his shoulder to point to the coracle, a small boat attached to the stern by a rope and carrying oars. I remembered seeing it when we had boarded. It seemed frail, made of some kind of wooden hoops covered with what looked like horsehide. Sam and his helper held the coracle as we climbed over the side and got in. When Sam joined us, I feared the little boat would sink.

Sam laughed and started rowing. "Don't worry yer head, this craft has held bigger loads." When we disembarked, he called, "Remember, down the road a piece and then turn right into the line of trees. Well, it's off to Dunquerque now."

Pierre knew Dunquerque well and took us swiftly to a stable, where we mounted horses for our brief journey to the dungeon. As we trotted south on the road lined with familiar poplar trees on each side, I felt a sudden pang. We were on French soil now, and although Toulouse lay many days' journey to the south, even the garb and chatter of the stable boys were sharp reminders that I had come home again.

The road to the dungeon ran fairly close to the waters of the Channel. As we rode, we could smell the salt air and hear the crash of the waves on the rocky shore. Pierre, who was in the lead, suddenly pulled his horse to

a halt and pointed. "Look!"

Outlined against the horizon was an immense stone building, topped by a wall with battlements like a castle's. Over the surrounding outside wall, I could see what looked like slits for windows and the top of a massive iron door in the center. We had reached the fortress.

We sat silent, staring at the dark bulk under the cloudy skies, with the gray-green waters lapping at its base. Were the others' hearts beginning to pump like mine? The plan I had worked out in Oxford had seemed so clever to me then. Suddenly I was full of misgivings—so many things could go wrong. Were we embarking on a foolhardy mission? Was I the only coward in the group?

Then I remembered how Roger Bacon had smiled when I stammered to him my fears that he might end up facing death at the stake. He had gone ahead with his experiment, refusing to let danger stop him.

If he could take such chances, so could I.

CHAPTER FOURTEEN

We rode up to the gate in the wall. Pierre reached over and rang the big iron bell that hung there. For a long moment, nothing happened. Finally, the great iron door beyond slowly creaked open and a man's figure appeared, shadowy in the distance.

The door was a good fifty paces or more from the gate. It was not until the man came nearer that we could see he was an armed soldier. Resting the butt of his halberd on the ground, he peered through the gate bars.

"Who are you? What want you here?" He spoke in French.

Pierre gave him a haughty stare. "I am Cardinal Cesarini, an emissary of the Holy Office in Rome. Take me to the warden of this prison."

Whether it was Pierre's commanding attitude or the mention of the Holy Office, the man put his weapon aside and hastened to unbar the gate. We rode in, Pierre leading, and dismounted.

"I'll call for a groom for your horses, sir."

"No need," snapped Pierre, "my man-at-arms here will take care of them. Our errand is short. We shall be leaving soon."

The soldier bowed and held the iron door open for us. "This way, sire."

The office of the warden was not far from the door. Stepping in, the soldier announced us. "Visitors from Rome, sir. From the Holy Office."

My experience with the Inquisitor had taught me well. Those two words—Holy Office—struck terror into the heart of anyone who heard them spoken. The warden, a short, stocky man wearing the robe of a Franciscan, virtually leapt to his feet from the chair behind his desk.

"The Holy Office? Rome? To what do we owe the pleasure of this visit?"

Pierre thrust the scroll of parchment at him. "This will explain all."

The warden unrolled the scroll and began to read. When he finished, he looked up at Pierre in astonishment. "Roger Bacon? But he's barely begun to serve his

sentence! His papers said at least ten years, I can show you. I don't understand."

I had coached Pierre well in the ways of the Holy Office. He strode forward and leaned over the desk, forcing the warden to gaze up into his face. "It is not our duty to understand, Warden, but to obey! Do you not see the seal at the bottom of that scroll? What does it say? Read it aloud!"

Fear made the warden stutter. "*Imp-imp-imprimatur s-si videbiture Reverendis P. Magistro Sacri Palatii Apostolico—*"

Pierre scowled. "In case your Latin is lacking, that means 'the seal you see is that of the Reverend High Magistrate of the Holy Apostolic Office'! Do you wish to question its authenticity?"

Pierre's tone seemed to shrivel the warden. He staggered back, almost falling into his chair. His eyes swiveled wildly from Pierre to me. I shook my head from side to side, and he got the message. "No, Your Eminence, the order is quite clear." He straightened up and rang the small bell on his desk. "Get me the keys to section nine," he ordered the clerk who came scurrying in.

Section nine proved to be the gloomy top floor of the prison. We followed the warden up three dark flights of narrow stairs. There were no windows for daylight to enter; the long corridor at the top was lighted at intervals by torches thrust into sconces. By each torch was a door, closed and flush with the wall. At eye level at the center

of each door was a metal slide. Three men standing guard in the corridor hurried toward us when they saw the warden.

"Anything wrong, sir?" asked one. They were all heavily armed with swords and halberds.

"No, no," replied the warden. "Uh—do you know which cell contains a certain Roger Bacon?" He moistened his lips.

"You mean the one who came in last?" The soldier jerked a thumb over his shoulder. "He's in number four."

As we followed the warden, the guards fell in behind us. I caught them eyeing Ian, who towered over them. At the door with *IV* painted on it, the warden stopped, moved the metal slide to one side, revealing a small opening, and peered in. "He's in there, all right." He fished through the ring of keys in his hands, selected one, thrust it in the lock, turned it, and pushed. Slowly, with a raspy creak of protest from rusted hinges, the iron door swung open.

There was scarcely enough daylight from the slit in the outside wall to see. I reached up, pulled one of the torches from its sconce, and followed the warden into the cell. In the flickering light, we could see the figure of a man slumped in one corner. I felt something touch my foot and looked down in time to spot a rat streaking for the door. The floor was covered with filthy straw that crunched under our feet.

As we moved closer, the man in the corner looked up.

Master Roger Bacon's eyes gazed into mine. Did a faint flicker of recognition narrow his lids? I brought my finger quickly to my lips, hoping he would understand the command to be silent.

Pierre played his part to the hilt. "Get him up!" he ordered the guards. They came forward and dragged Master Bacon to his feet. Chains locked to his wrists and ankles clanked on the floor. "Are you Roger Bacon, late of Oxford University?"

Master Bacon's face turned from me to Pierre. His mouth opened. I prayed he would not cry out his friend's name. To my relief, he seemed to grasp the situation. "Yes, I am." He spoke with an effort.

I stared at the master, who kept blinking in the sudden flood of light from the torch. It was only a matter of weeks since I had seen him, but he was barely recognizable. His uncombed hair had much more white than I remembered. An unkempt white beard covered the lower part of his face. And that face, so glowing and full of life before, now had sunken cheeks streaked by deep lines. Manacles on his arms and legs were connected to long chains fastened to one wall.

"Get those chains off him!" Pierre's commanding tone made the warden begin at once to fumble through his keys until he found the right one. Bacon's chains fell with a crash to the ground. "Master Roger Bacon," Pierre continued, "you are hereby summoned to accompany us to Rome, to stand before the Holy Office and defend the accusation of heresy. Do you understand?" Bacon nodded. "Good." He turned to Ian. "Take him out."

Ian lifted Bacon gently and put an arm about him to lead him toward the door. At first, Bacon's feet seemed not to obey him—he stumbled, recovered, and would have fallen without Ian's strong grasp. Then he began to move with little steps. As Ian took him past us and out of the cell, Pierre's back was to the warden. I caught a quick wink of Pierre's eye at Bacon. Still holding the torch, I followed them out into the corridor. The warden and his guards stood watching us.

To my surprise, two Franciscan friars barred our way. "Warden," one of them called, "will you come here, please?"

Pierre turned and frowned at the warden. "Who are those brothers?"

"Members of my staff. I'll just see what they want." He pushed past us and walked over to the friars. One of them whispered in his ear. Whatever was going on, I did not like it. While my right hand kept the torch upright, my left crept toward the pouch under my robe. With my eyebrows, I sent Ian a signal to be careful. He nodded imperceptibly and moved one hand onto the pommel of his sword.

The warden came back to Pierre, his mouth working.

"What's the delay?" asked Pierre. "Let us proceed at once!"

"Is it possible," said the warden loudly, "that you are

not a representative of the Holy Office at all, but a Franciscan known to all as Petrus Peregrinus?"

"What?" Pierre may have been caught by surprise, but he recovered instantly. "What kind of nonsense is this? Do you wish me to report your insolence to the Grand Inquisitor?"

The warden pointed. "That man tells me he was one of your companions when you roamed the countryside with the goliards. And I believe him!" Turning to the guards behind Ian and Bacon, he cried, "Take them!"

"Stop!" I shouted. "Wait! You forget what this man Bacon can do! He's a magician with marvelous powers!" The men froze in their tracks. Meanwhile, I was putting the long cylinder that Johannus had prepared into the flame of the torch. "This man can call up the Devil, who comes in a flash of flame and smoke to do his bidding!"

At that moment, I heard the brief sizzle and threw the saltpeter roll at the feet of the guards. "Come on," I yelled to Ian and Pierre, "follow me!" The last word had barely left my lips when there was a huge explosion. The flash of flame and the cloud of smoke, followed by the crash of thunder, sent the warden and his men staggering back.

"Take care," cried one of the friars, "it's the fires of Hell!" In a high, shaky voice, he began a prayer invoking God's help against Satan.

Pierre dashed past me, pushed the trembling friars to one side, and took Bacon's arm from Ian. Grabbing the other arm, I helped Pierre hurry him down the corridor

toward the stairwell. There another guard blocked the way. But I thrust the torch into his face, and he fell back.

"On with ye, lads!" shouted Ian. "I'll keep 'em off yer backs. It's easy odds, only five against one!"

His words cheered us on as we hauled Bacon down the stairs. Up in the corridor we had just left, I could hear the warden screaming, "Sound the alarm! Sound the alarm!"

By the time we reached the first floor, bells were ringing all over the prison. As we emerged from the stairwell and turned left toward the front door, I glanced back down the corridor. What looked like a small army was advancing toward us, swords and halberds flashing in the torchlight.

Dismay surged through me. Pierre had been right—it was impossible. We'd never make it out the door.

But just then I heard the voice of Ian behind me. "Keep going, lads! I'll handle these scroungy blackguards!"

At the sight of Ian's huge frame, the guards in the lead slowed their pace. Without looking back, Pierre and I lifted Bacon off his feet and carried him to the massive door. As I released Bacon's arm to open the door, I could hear the clash of sword on sword behind us. Under my breath, I found myself muttering a prayer for Ian's safety. Finally we were outside in the blessed salt air.

With a flash of panic, I remembered the soldier who had stayed out there with Giles. Surely by now he would have heard the alarm bells. How on earth would we deal

with him?

But I needn't have worried. There was Giles with the horses, quite safe, with the soldier's halberd in his hands. And there was the soldier, unarmed, sitting dejectedly on the ground. As we came toward him, Giles kept the sharp blade of the halberd at the soldier's neck. I heard him saying, "One move from you, and..."

Pierre slung Bacon onto his horse's back and leapt into the saddle behind him. I dropped the torch and jumped on my horse. "Where's Ian?" called Giles.

I turned my head. "Holding them back!"

"You go ahead. I'll wait and see if Ian needs help."

Leaving Giles behind while I rode to safety made me uneasy. Hadn't I promised his mother to watch out for him? But how could I help without a decent weapon? And it was my job to find the cove for Pierre, who was burdened with Bacon.

At the front gate, I leapt off my horse, removed the bar, and swung the gate open. Pierre trotted through, and I remounted and followed. Once outside, we whipped our horses to a gallop. For a second I looked back. Then a turn in the road cut the prison off from sight. Oh, dear God, I thought, why didn't I just grab that soldier's halberd back there and stay behind to fight? Giles had his own sword; we could have both helped Ian! But it was too late now. Pierre was already well ahead of me.

"Pierre," I yelled, "slow down! We have to give the others a chance to catch up." I wouldn't let myself think that Ian and Giles would never make it.

Our gallop became a canter and then a trot. "Let's turn off and wait behind this thicket," said Pierre, turning his horse off the road.

I dismounted and helped Bacon down from Pierre's saddle. "Are you all right, Master Bacon?"

He leaned against a tree trunk. "I'd do better sitting down." He slid to a sitting position. "By the good Lord. . ." Bacon shook his head in amazement. "When Pierre began all that nonsense about the Inquisition"—he heaved a sigh—"and I was able to get a good look at you two, I couldn't believe my eyes."

"I was praying you wouldn't blurt out my name," said Pierre. "Not that I would have blamed you. We must've been quite a surprise."

"More like a shock. But I caught Jean's motion to be silent, and then when I saw him light that saltpeter thunderbolt—"

"Wait," I broke in. "Listen." I put up a hand to cup my ear. "Hoofbeats, can you hear?" I moved out toward the road and took shelter behind a tree. Peering out, I could make out two horsemen galloping toward me. My heart raced till they came closer. At last, one of them was unmistakable, and I ran back to the thicket. "They're coming! Ian and Giles made it out!" Thankfulness washed over me like a welcome rain.

We helped Bacon back up onto Pierre's horse, then we rode out onto the road just as Ian and Giles drew up.

"Och, lads," shouted Ian, "better move on! By now they'll be mounted and after us!" While I ached to know what had happened back at the prison, it was no time for stories. Side by side, we quickly urged our horses to a fast gallop.

Pierre turned his head toward me. "Where do we turn to get to that cove?"

I had taken care to note something about the growth behind the beach when Seabury sailed into the cove to show us the spot. "I remember two of the poplars that were not quite straight, they leaned into each other. Watch for them on our right."

About fifty paces farther along, Pierre pointed. "There, up ahead. Are those the trees?"

I squinted and then nodded yes. We motioned to Ian and Giles to turn off with us. Once clear of the road, Ian sprang from his horse. "You hide in the underbrush here. I'll take the horses back where they can't be seen from the road. Don't move, lads, till they've gone by." After we dismounted, he took the four bridles and disappeared with the horses in the direction of the cove.

Ian was right. After a few minutes, I could hear the sound of pounding horses' hooves approaching. The pounding became louder and louder, until a squadron of about twenty mounted soldiers swept past our hiding place.

Pierre signaled with a wave. The three of us rose and made for the cove as quickly as we could through the thick underbrush. Giles tried to hold back tree branches as Pierre and I carried Bacon along. As the underbrush thinned, I caught a glimpse of the rippling water beyond. Ian was waiting there with the horses. And like the miracle we needed, there was Sam Seabury, sitting on the sand next to his coracle.

When Sam spotted us, he leaped to his feet. "Into the boat with ye!" he cried, and moved the coracle into the water. First we helped Bacon sit in the stern, then the rest of us found places. It was a tight fit, especially when Ian hopped in after helping Sam push the coracle out into deeper water. But the rim of the boat remained above the waterline, and Sam quickly rowed us toward the *London Belle* lying at anchor.

A sudden hullabaloo made us turn our heads. The pursuing squadron had somehow gotten wind of our whereabouts. They were standing at the water's edge, shouting and waving their weapons. A few of them seemed to be jumping up and down in a rage because their prey was lost.

"Looks like ye were runnin' a tight race there," drawled Sam, as he stood and caught hold of the ship's rail. "Wouldn't care to meet up with them fellers myself. Now I'll hold on to this while ye climb over one by one. Mind ye, don't push too hard and dump us all into the sea."

Sam's mate was waiting for us. I got a leg up over the rail first, and he helped me over. Together we hauled

Master Bacon onto the deck. When we were all safely aboard, Sam handed me the coracle's rope. "Walk her around to the stern and tie her back while we get the sail up."

Moments later Sam was steering the *London Belle* north into the Strait of Dover. I stood in the stern next to Sam and looked back. The soldiers on the beach were diminishing in size, until they were only little mechanical dolls dancing about. And then they were lost beyond the horizon.

We had won. The impossible had become possible.

CHAPTER FIFTEEN

As our ship tacked toward Margate and the mouth of the Thames, we sat on the deck in a circle around Roger Bacon. He lay with his back against the forecastle wall, his face turned toward the sun. Color had begun to return to his cheeks, so that even the lines around his eyes and mouth seemed less harsh.

"Tell us, how did you manage to get that soldier's weapon?" I asked Giles.

Giles laughed. "It was easy. I was wearing a sword, remember, so he figured I was a fellow soldier. Talked about how he was just back from one of the Crusades.

So I told him I'd never used a halberd before and asked if he'd show me how. Once I had the halberd in my hands, the rest was easy."

Battles were nothing new to Ian, a member of the Northern Nation. He regaled us with a description of his skirmish down the corridor with the guards. "Och, it started with that gang up there on the third floor. I didn't even have to use my sword! After I banged a few heads together, they lost their taste for fighting."

"But what about the guards we saw rushing down the corridor just as we went out the door?" Pierre was shaking his head as if he couldn't believe what Ian was saying.

"Och, that was more like it—ten to one—made the fighting a bit spicier. What the relief troops didn't realize was that the corridor was too narrow for more than two to come at me at the same time. See, the cutthroats behind had to climb over the bodies of the ones already kissed by my sword. Och, it was a grand fight, I tell ye, lads!"

Bacon, who had not spoken a word since we sailed from the cove, opened his mouth. "By God, Pierre, it sounds as though you got the entire Scottish army to come to my rescue!"

"Not I," Pierre replied. "It's this young friar, Jean of Toulouse, you should thank. The whole thing was his idea."

Bacon turned his head. "I thank you, Jean."

"But Master Bacon," I asked, "why did they arrest you?

What were the grounds?"

"Does the Holy Office ever need grounds?" Bacon's mouth twisted. "My guess is that Thomas of York persuaded them to get my own order to condemn me. It must have been the saltpeter demonstration that did me in."

"I think you're right. It was all too sudden, too new. The authorities must have been frightened." The demonstration and the panic it caused had worried me from the start.

"But still," Bacon laughed, "I see you used my invention to good advantage."

We all joined in the laughter. "Nevertheless," Pierre pointed out, "we now have to consider what to do. Roger, you can't just show up at the university. Once Thomas of York knows you're back, he'll not hesitate to find out if your release was official. No, you'll have to go into hiding until—"

"Hiding? "Bacon interrupted. "Hiding? I'll not hide from ignorance and stupidity! Nor from this idiotic charge of heresy! I'll demand a fair trial and show them that my science has nothing to do with their superstitious fears!"

Bacon's toughness after what he had been through amazed me. "Forgive me, Master Bacon, but we mustn't underestimate the way the Holy Office works. Their ideas of truth and honesty are not like yours! Remember how they used me to incriminate you. They'll go to any extreme to see you returned to that dungeon. Or worse."

"Jean is right," said Pierre. "It would be foolhardy to come forward and demand a fair trial. You'll have to lay low until we can find some authority willing to come to your defense."

Ian suddenly spoke up. "Why, lads, if there's no objection, yon Master Bacon is welcome to be my guest at Inverness. Keep in mind, I'm now the laird. Nobody will dare to take him out of my castle without my permission!"

"Good idea, Ian," put in Giles. "And first you can all stay in my house till Master Bacon feels strong enough to make the journey."

Bacon's eyes searched out our faces and suddenly blurred with tears. "Pierre—" He stopped to wipe his eyes with a sleeve. "Pierre, I thought you and Johannus were the only true friends I had. And now I can count three more."

"Then it's decided." Pierre sounded relieved. "So I'll soon be off to try my hand at a new quest."

Bacon raised a hand. "One provision, however. On the way to Scotland we must stop at Oxford. We must let Johannus know I am safe."

Pierre and I looked at each other. "There's no need, Master," I said. "We can send a message to Johannus—"

"No, no!" Bacon waved his hand feebly. "I must get to my laboratory, see if everything's all right."

I nodded. "We can manage to smuggle you in and out for that."

Bacon smiled. But the exertion of talking had tired him. His eyes closed, his head tipped to one side, and he slept. Night had fallen by the time the *London Belle* docked.

As our horses trotted through the gate and into the courtyard of Giles's house, the front door opened and Giles's mother appeared. With a cry of joy, she ran toward us. In a moment, Giles was off his horse and in her arms.

"Welcome, welcome all!" she cried as soon as the embrace ended.

"Madame Rowley, this is Master Roger Bacon." Pierre had helped Bacon off his horse. "Roger, this is Giles's mother, whose kindness surpasses all."

Bacon took her hand. "Dame Rowley, I owe your brave son a debt of gratitude."

"You are a welcome guest, Master Bacon. Please come in, you must be exhausted."

What took place during the following days was the restoration of Roger Bacon to the man I had first met at Oxford. Giles's mother treated Bacon as she had probably treated Giles as a child when he came in from play. First came a hot bath and a complete change of clothes. "Take this filth," she ordered the servant who picked up Bacon's dungeon clothing, "and burn it!"

Giles brought Bacon his father's razor, and the white beard disappeared. Another servant scissored Bacon's long hair into a neat pattern. At Bacon's order, he also razored clean the pate of Bacon's head. "Though the Franciscans seem to have betrayed me," Bacon told us,

"I will not betray my vows."

"Into bed with you," commanded the mistress of the house, and I was surprised to see how meekly this bold philosopher obeyed.

On the morning of the fourth day, Bacon threw aside the bedclothes and announced that it was time to stop imposing on these fine people. He was ready to ride to Oxford, or even to the ends of the earth if he had to. Neither Dame Rowley's protestations nor ours made the slightest dent in his confidence. Two days later, the four of us—Bacon, Pierre, Ian, and I—said our farewells to the Rowleys.

"Mind you," Giles said to Ian and me, "I'll expect to hear from you if any new adventure crops up."

"Aye, lad, that you will," agreed Ian.

"For my part," I told Giles, "if you want a new adventure, come back to Oxford and help me bone up on all the lectures I've missed." His answer was a solid poke in my ribs.

A last fond look back at Giles and his mother waving to us, and I was out the gate and away.

Though Bacon sat his horse well, it was obvious that trying to ride at a fast pace would tire him too soon. We settled for a fast trot along the road to Oxford, which meant that we would not be there until the following day. At sundown, we found an inn and took adjoining rooms.

"Roger," said Pierre, as we sat at supper, "if you are determined to stop at the university, we'll have to find

a way to disguise your appearance."

"Och, I have it." Ian took a swallow of ale and continued. "There's an extra tunic in my pack. Ye can doff your robe and look like a soldier."

The three of us considered this idea for a moment. I looked at Bacon's head. "But what kind of soldier wears a friar's shaven pate?"

"Och, ye're sharp tonight, laddie." Ian cut himself a chunk of meat, chewed, and swallowed. "Now that I think of it, there's a soft campaign hat in my pack, too."

"Splendid, Ian, you've saved the day!"

So it was two friars and two soldiers who rode through the open gate of Oxford University the next day. At the sight of the green quadrangle, my heart gave a leap. I hadn't been sure I would ever see it again.

We left our horses at the university stables and walked across to the laboratory. The door was closed. When Bacon tried to open it, he found it was locked.

"How can this be? Where is Johannus?" In his dismay, Bacon banged his fist on the door.

With a slight creak, the door cracked open and an eye peered out at us. We heard a yelp of joy. The door was flung wide. It was Johannus, eyes sparkling, mouth spread in a grin. "Master Bacon, it's you!"

"Shhh! Quiet!" Pierre came forward, pushed Johannus back in the laboratory and motioned for us to enter quickly. The door slammed shut.

"Wh-what's the matter?" Johannus had a look of

utter confusion on his face.

"Don't you realize that Roger is a fugitive? No one must know he's here!"

"Fugitive? Then you don't know?"

"Know what, Johannus? What are you talking about?" Bacon seized Johannus by the front of his apron. "What is it we should know?"

"Yesterday. He came yesterday. A messenger from the Vatican. The pope—the pope—wait, he left a message!" Johannus wrenched himself free from Bacon's grasp and dashed over to the table. When he returned, a roll of parchment was in his hand. "Here!"

Bacon's hand trembled as he unrolled the parchment. As his eyes scanned the words, his mouth fell open.

"For God's sake, Roger, read it aloud before we perish," said Pierre.

"It says that Pope Clement IV, formerly Cardinal de Foulques, sends his personal regards to Master Roger Bacon of the Order of St. Francis. His Holiness has ordered that all accusations against me are to be dropped!"

Bacon began to read directly from the parchment. "'His Holiness also, being aware that Master Bacon has added much of value to our understanding of God's universe, bids Master Bacon collect whatever he has written of his ideas and to add to them any new writings he may wish to create. The said writings are to be collected in a single volume, copied in the scriptorium by the best copyists, and sent to His Holiness as soon as it is finished. Monies to pay for such work will be granted by us. Given on this day to my hand in the second year of the Julian calendar. *Deo gratias, Amen*. Clement IV.'"

We all stood there, stunned. Then, as though the same thought had popped into our heads at the same time, we seized hands and formed a ring around Bacon, dancing and shouting like children playing ring-around-the-rosy. In the center, Bacon stood laughing and crying at the same time. Finally he waved his hands and shouted, "Enough! Enough! Johannus, a flagon of ale! We must drink a toast to His Holiness!"

I could not resist the question. "Did you know His Holiness when he was a cardinal?"

"I did indeed! Long ago, before I came to Oxford, I lectured at Paris. The faculty there denounced me as a heretic—"

"I remember, I remember!" cried Pierre. "I was there! And de Foulques arose and defended you against all those idiots!"

"He was a fine honest man, and he was my friend." Bacon's voice became somber. "I can't bear it—I put all your lives in danger for nothing. They would have freed me from prison anyway."

"No!" It hurt me to see him so upset. "Who knows how long it would've taken them to carry out the order to free you! They could have conveniently forgotten about you for years! This way you are out and free. And we are none the worse for wear."

"Well, lads." Ian tossed off the last of his ale. "Looks like my invitation's gone agley. But it stands for all of ye. If ye wish to break away from this den of learnin' and follow a more useful pursuit like salmon fishin', ye're all welcome to Inverness any time."

He shook hands all around and turned to go. I felt sad to see that great mass of man leaving instead of arriving.

"Roger," said Pierre, "I congratulate you on your good news. You'd better get to work, and I'd better get going."

"Going? Going where, my friend?"

"You know me, Roger—once a wandering scholar, never fixed in place. I'm off to Egypt. Going to have a try at translating that strange picture writing of the ancients I've heard so much about. And you have to get to work and make His Holiness a happy man." He turned to me. "And you'd better stay here so you can help him, Jean. I must be off. Farewell—it was a magnificent adventure. Good-bye, Johannus."

Now the master and his two apprentices were alone. "Well, Jean, what are your plans for the future?"

I shrugged. "When Master Thomas told me of my release, he said I'd be welcome to study at the University of Paris. That's where I was supposed to go, you know, before—before all of this."

"Ah, yes, Paris. Well, it's not a bad school. Thomas Aquinas, you know."

"But, Master Roger—" began Johannus.

"Hush, Johannus, Jean must decide for himself."

Thomas Aquinas. And my own native land again. My chance to be closer to my family, now safe from the Inquisition. And to visit the abbey. France again. Home.

And yet—and yet...I looked at the magician and his apprentice. My eyes traveled around the laboratory walls, with the shelves stuffed with flasks and crucibles. And all those books. Johannus had moved away and was preparing to fire the furnace again.

Had the Grand Inquisitor of Toulouse unwittingly done me a favor, after all? It was in this room that I had begun to think for myself.

Roger Bacon stood there, his eyes boring into mine. And suddenly I knew the answer. I did not have to move an inch to go home.

I was already home.

AFTERWORD

This is a work of fiction. Many of the characters in it, as well as the events, are inventions of the storytellers' minds. But the entire story is padded around a skeleton of some truths we know about the time during which our tale takes place.

Most of what is known about Roger Bacon comes from his letters, those of his works that survived, and university and monastic records. He was a Franciscan monk who taught both at Oxford University and at the University of Paris. From the letter he wrote to a friend denying the existence of black magic and praising the "magic" to be learned from observing nature comes the anagram for the making of gunpowder (something the Chinese had already been using since the late 400s A.D.). The solution for the anagram, which may or may not be what Bacon intended, but seems right, is the work of an American historian of chemistry named Tenney L. Davis.

Whether or not Bacon actually gave a demonstration of his gunpowder to the faculty of Oxford is not certain, but he must have shown somebody there what happened when it exploded. However, science at that time was still mixed with magic and superstition. It's easy to understand how the authorities found the ideas and actions of such a scientist so frightening that they associated him with the powers of evil.

It was Bacon's own order, the Franciscans, who finally did imprison him in a dungeon on the coast of France.

Since he was considered by the Church to be a heretic, it is possible that the Inquisition played a part in his being jailed, though no proof of this exists. Pope Clement IV did order Bacon's writings to be collected and sent to him. But the pope died soon after, and Bacon's imprisonment followed. We storytellers sent our hero Jean and his friends to come to Bacon's rescue. What really happened is that Bacon languished in prison for about ten years before being released to return to Oxford.

The truth is that the ideas we had Bacon present in his lecture took over three hundred years to come to fruition in the publication of the work of Sir Francis Bacon of Elizabethan England (no relation). Pierre de Maricourt (Petrus Peregrinus) was also a real person, and he did bring the magnetic compass to the West, probably from the Islamic world (where it had come from China). And the battle of Lewes really was fought between King Henry III and his barons, led by Simon de Montfort.

We trust the reader will not fret over the few liberties we have taken with some of the facts of history. We hope our student characters and their adventures give the reader a picture of university life in that early period. Roger Bacon's struggle typifies the cultural blocks that faced any scientist of his day who dared to be different.